NIGHT OF THE BAT

Also by Paul Zindel

The P.C. Hawke Mysteries
Rats
Raptor
Reef of Death
The Doom Stone
Loch

NIGHT OF THE BAT

PAUL ZINDEL

HYPERION
NEW YORK

First Edition
1 3 5 7 9 10 8 6 4 2
This book is set in 13.5-point Bembo.
Printed in the United States of America

Library of Congress Cataloging-in-Publication Data
Zindel, Paul.
Night of the bat / Paul Zindel.
p. cm.
Summary: Teenage Jake joins his father on an expedition to study bats in the Brazilian
rain forest and finds the project menaced by a giant brain-eating bat.
ISBN 0-7868-0340-1 (hc.)—ISBN 0-7868-2554-5 (lib. bdg.)
[1. Bats—Fiction. 2. Monsters—Fiction. 3. Brazil—Fiction. 4. Amazon River
Region—Fiction.] I. Title.

PZ7.Z647 Ni 2001
[Fic]—dc21
Visit www.hyperionteens.com

Dedicated to Dorothy Ames and our Milford dinners over which we discuss the labyrinths and flights of Family.

CONTENTS

NIGHT OF THE BAT

1 • EMERGENCE

Jake heard the small mammal sounds erupting from the end of the high ramp where the vines swirled to form a cave. There came the flutter of wings, and the nightly emergence had begun: a blanket of glistening bats—hundreds of bats!—with bulldoglike ears and tiny, punched-in faces.

Bats flying right at Jake.

Jake called down from the canopy to his dad, on the jungle floor. "Send the sling up for me. Now, Dad, *now.*"

He tried to escape, but it was too late. The wave of bats swelled and began to wash up over his legs. They bit at his ankles, small razor cuts from short, feeding jaws.

"Help me! Dad!" he shrieked.

Jake drew in air to scream. A living, furry scarf scampered up to cover his mouth. One of the bats tore at his lips, then shimmied its small hairy head and legs and wing tips inside of his mouth. He tried to yell as it crawled violently, deep into his throat.

A small head.

Biting inside him.

Jake screaming. Screaming and praying and . . .

"Wake up, young man. Excuse me. Wake up."

Jake Lefkovitz's eyes snapped open. He realized that the flight attendant was shaking him by the shoulder.

"Oh . . . sorry," Jake said, bolting upright in his window seat on the M-80 jetliner.

"Please put your seat back forward and make certain your safety belt is secure," the flight attendant said. She smiled. "We'll be landing in Manaus in twenty minutes."

Jake noticed that several of the passengers were staring at him. He knew he must have cried out. The remnants of the nightmare were like snakes turning in the back of his mind. "I dreamed my allowance got cut," he announced, laughing and rapping his knuckles on his head like a clown.

He knew he had stayed up too long the night

before. For weeks, he'd spent hours at the New York Public Library reading like a demon everything he could get his hands on about bats and the Amazon. He'd read books and magazines from the Smithsonian. A colleague of his father's had lent him videos and audiotapes from the Museum of Natural History. One was about batologists like his father, working high in the rain forest canopy of Brazil. The other was about the wildlife—capybaras, deadly anacondas. Army ants cutting a ten-foot swath through the jungle.

On this trip, Jake was determined to prove himself to his dad, who thought Jake couldn't take anything seriously. It was true that he had a reputation as a joker, that he liked a good laugh. Now he wanted to show he had grown up and changed—that he could be part of his father's research team and act responsibly.

Jake looked out the plane window as it circled low over Manaus, the capital of the Amazonas state. From the air it appeared to be an oasis of broad streets and plazas in the middle of a belt of greedy jungle—part of a lush wilderness territory as big as the United States. When the plane landed, the flight attendant kept her eye on him.

"I'm okay," Jake said. "I always yell in my sleep."

"How strange," the flight attendant said.

His face reddened. He covered his embarrassment with a wink as he got his overstuffed duffel bag, a heavy cardboard box bound with rope, and a big aluminum boom box down from a storage compartment. He put a small bag of peanut-butter cookies saved from the in-flight dinner into the duffel bag. Peanut-butter cookies had always been his favorite, and they had been, by far, the best thing about the meal. He lugged his carry-ons to the open doorway, where the heat socked him like a hammer.

As he came down the stair ramp, it was easy for him to spot the guide his father had sent to meet him. A tiny, wrinkled man with waist-length gray hair waited alone on the tarmac.

"Welcome to Manaus, Master Jake," the man said as he extended his hand. "I'm Hanuma, your father's foreman."

"*Ciao,*" Jake said, taking Hanuma's thin, stiff hand and shaking it. "'*Ciao*' is Italian for hello and good-bye."

"I see." Hanuma stared at him and took his hand back. "I have a taxi waiting to take us to the river dock," he said, leading the way through the small, stifling, terminal and out an exit to the pickup area.

Jake felt the tropic heat deep in his lungs now, and he remembered he was heading into a jungle where men perish. "Did you ever find the missing men from the expedition?" Jake asked.

"No . . ."

"It's a little scary, isn't it? When Dad called last week, he sounded really worried about them. Is it possible they just got bored and took off?"

Hanuma grunted. "My workers do not *take off*," he said. "The missing men are the main reason Dr. Lefkovitz didn't want you to come out to the camp. He said you should stay in Manaus, and he can join you down here at the end of the month. See the Theatro. The museums. There will be time for a safe tour of the river before the rains come."

"No way," Jake said. "I'm going back upriver with you guys. Dad's been gone too long. If something weird is going on out at his camp, I don't want him doing a disappearing act, too. Guys don't just disappear from my dad's expeditions. Even my mom's worried and wants him to pack it in."

"Then why didn't she come?"

"Well, she's with a law firm and is still busy clawing her way to the top. She lay around the house for a couple of decades, and now you can't stop her. Last week her firm sent her to Tonga. I don't even know where that is."

"That explains it," Hanuma said.

"What?"

"Why you are in Manaus despite your father's warning. You just do whatever you want." Hanuma smiled, flashing a gold front tooth.

"That was the old me," Jake said. "Dad never let me get away with too much. You know how he wants things done his way. I think one of the reasons I've come down here is to let him know I found out he was usually right."

Hanuma glanced up toward the equatorial sun. "Ah, I understand you now. You want your father to see that you have learned to be wise and have courage. My seventeen sons and daughters were like you when they were young. Full of themselves. Maybe you will learn—as your father should have—that sometimes, in the Amazon," he said seriously, "it is a fine thing if one can admit they are wrong. Or it can be 'Ciao, baby' forever."

2 • THE RIVER

The taxi driver, a young Indian wearing a grime-stained baseball cap and a T-shirt, left the side of his beat-up Ford station wagon, and helped Jake put his luggage into the trunk. Jake kept his CD player with him.

"What is in the big cardboard box?" Hanuma asked Jake.

"Some electrical thingamajig. I did my science project on echolocation—bat radar. Some pretty interesting stuff. I figured Dad would want to see it."

"Perhaps," Hanuma said, as he and Jake slid into the backseat. "Do you mind if I ask why you didn't stay home in New York City and eat ice cream and pizzas? Maybe make an appointment to see your mother and let her buy you more Gap jeans and Tommy shirts?"

"Thanks," Jake said. "You sound like you've been to the States a lot."

"Enough to know that an air-conditioned mall is more fun than the jungles of Jurua Lace. And safer."

"Safer I don't know about," Jake said. "We've got our share of savages running around Manhattan, too, you know. How long's the trip to Dad's camp?"

"A small moon and fourteen waterfalls."

"Is that like half past a jaguar's a—?"

Hanuma cut him off. "Dr. Lefkovitz warned me that you would be a very silly boy."

"Thank you. I *am* the only one in our family that still has a sense of humor."

"If that's what you want to call it," Hanuma said. "Dr. Lefkovitz says you can be a real teenage pain in the butt."

"How's that for PR?"

Hanuma sighed.

As the taxi left the center of Manaus, the elaborate fountains and statues of the plazas gave way to narrow streets of makeshift Indian stores and checkerboard gardens. Several tourist cafes with striped awnings and neon signs lined the riverbank near the main deep-water dock. Gaudy tour boats were moored side by side small fishing skiffs and beached narrow dugouts called *pirogues*.

The driver pulled the taxi to a halt at one of the small Indian docks. Two well-built men in loincloths left their freshly stocked pirogue and helped Jake with his duffel bag and box of rattling electronics.

By the time Hanuma had finished haggling with the driver over the fare, the men were ready to launch the pirogue onto the river.

Jake knew his father had sent his best men to bring him upriver: Hanuma and two Indians who had made the journey many times. They ordered Jake to sit between Muras, the bowman with the supplies, and Hanuma's main man, Dangari. Hanuma squatted at the back of the pirogue where he could help steer. Jake knew from his father's letters that Hanuma was able to troubleshoot most of his expedition's problems. He'd once been a shaman in the Murdaruci tribe, and was said to have special gifts, like clairvoyance.

He knows across great distances, without phone or walkie-talkie, when one of his men or children has been bit by a snake or fallen from a tree, Dr. Lefkovitz had written. *That is why the workers missing from the camp* are *of great concern to us. Hanuma believes something bad has happened to them. He can no longer feel their spirits.*

Muras and Dangari were like most of the men from the Murdaruci tribe, olive-skinned, short, but with powerful builds and lustrous straight black hair like that of cliff divers. Under Hanuma's orders, they cut their paddles with the sharpness of knives into the dark river water, and used them to steer in the rapids. The whole first day there was always the distant sound of screeching chain saws and roaring earthmovers. Swaths of mahogany rain forest were being cleared as far as the eye could see. Lumber trucks with poisonous fumes coughing from their cab pipes tore along dirt roads like ruthless juggernauts.

As dusk set in, the sky reddened and the banks along a tributary of the river were unspoiled jungle again.

Hanuma picked their camping spot for the night and supervised the raising of the tents and the making of a fire. Dinner was slicings from a slab of salted tapir.

The next morning, Jake helped shove off into rapids that threatened to capsize the pirogue. At each waterfall, he pitched in with the Indians to carry the long dugout and supplies carefully up to the next stretch of flat, slower river. When it was calm, Jake played rock CDs on his boom box—and once, some loud rap just to see the look on Hanuma's face.

"I see you are trying to drive me and the jungle crazy," Hanuma said.

"Oh, you mean the music?" Jake asked.

"Yes. The racket."

A constant mist drifted down through the towering trees and walls of vines. The main waters of the entire Amazon basin were born in the Andes. Soon, when the high mountain snows melted, they would violently flood the area as they did every year.

"How much time before the flooding starts at the camp?" Jake asked.

"Soon," Hanuma said. "Maybe a couple of weeks. The waters will rise quickly and fish will swim in the forest," Hanuma said, his voice gentle with a mix of Portuguese and Indian accents. "Within a month, giant water ferns will arise where your father's camp now stands. There will be too many piranha to keep away with the sound of his old truck motor. River dolphins have begun to play near the camp falls, and the spider monkeys are already chattering nervously. Yes, the high water is coming."

"Has Dad collected a lot of nifty bats?" Jake asked.

"Plenty, if you ask me. He always wants to find more. He makes Muras draw them. Muras can draw very well."

"Dad told me he's after vampires on this trip," Jake said. "They're really nasty little suckers, aren't they?"

"Yes," Hanuma said.

"I've seen them in the nocturnal room at the Bronx Zoological Gardens," Jake said. "The staff puts out petri dishes of cow's blood for them to lap up."

"The north jungle has many of the 'little suckers,' as you say, that your father wants to study," Hanuma said. "They sleep in the vines and hollowed tree trunks during the day. At night, they fly to feast on the backs of monkeys and wild boars. My men wake up sometimes to see bats drinking blood from their own legs and faces."

"In that case, I guess there won't be much sack time for me." Jake remembered his dream on the plane, and his stomach tightened. Perhaps he'd read too much about bats. The gentle way they bite. How they can give someone a fatal disease without their even knowing. "Isn't anyone afraid of getting rabies?"

"That is a danger, too," Hanuma said. "You go crazy. It is a terrible death. But my men are more afraid of a puma attack or cayman alligators grabbing them in the river and eating them. Here the alligators kill and hide their prey beneath mounds of underwater peat."

The idea was disturbing to Jake, but he had no intention of showing fear. "Great marinade," he said.

"My tribesmen are also afraid of evil tree spirits and mountain lightning—and tiny barbed catfish that can swim up into their body cavities."

Jake decided not even to think about that.

It was afternoon by the time they reached Dark Angel Falls. Jake helped carry the pirogue and supplies up the towering, steep rocky bank to a cove above the falls. In the last hours of the journey, the river narrowed to less than a hundred feet wide and its water became clear. Electric eels and iridescent neon fish flashed in the eddies. A jaguar watched them from high in a tree as they passed. Tapirs and capybaras drank at the riverbank.

Jake noticed spiderwebs with strands as thick as cord. Once, when the pirogue had to pass under an overhang of tropical willows, ticks the size of acorns and large clawed beetles rained down and had to be brushed into the river.

As the sun began to set, Hanuma called out. "There's your father."

3 • STRANGERS

Jake could hardly recognize the man waiting for them in the mist at the landing. His dad looked thinner than Jake had ever seen him. It was always a shock to see him after he'd spent a few months in the jungle. By now he had a full beard, and his eyes were puffy. He wore a tan pith helmet to shield his balding head. There were always changes inside, too. Changes in the way he thought. Secrets from each expedition.

A handful of Indian workers flanked Dr. Lefkovitz on the small area that had been cleared at the river' bank. They helped beach the pirogue. As Jake disembarked he could see that the camp wasn't much larger than a baseball diamond, carved out of the heavy foliage and giant grandiflora and mahogany trees of the rain forest.

Three huts and a half dozen thatched lean-tos had been erected in a circle. Clusters of ropes and pulleys spiraled skyward as though the entire camp were controlled by the strings of a puppet master.

"I wish you hadn't come, son," was the first thing out of Dr. Lefkovitz's mouth. He extended his hand as if he were greeting a stranger.

For a moment, Jake surprised himself with his own sudden anger. He realized he wanted to yell at his father, *Are those the only words you can think to say to me? You haven't seen me in months, and that's what you've got to say!*

"Pops, I know you don't want me hanging around here," Jake said. "You never want me on any of your bat treks."

"If only you could ever take anything seriously," his father said, seeing the CD player Jake clutched like a suitcase.

"Hey, I've spent the last couple of months studying bats. I'll know what you're talking about. This time I can help. I'll move equipment. Build huts. I'm stronger. I was on the track and gymnastic teams at

Dalton. I ran in Central Park. Worked out at the gym. You'll see . . ."

"Jake, what I need you to be is a team player. The men won't accept a selfish fool on this expedition."

"I'm not a selfish fool," Jake said. "Not anymore."

Muras and Dangari brought Jake's things to the main hut. Hanuma gave Jake his cardboard box. "Your son did well on the journey here," Hanuma told Dr. Lefkovitz.

Dr. Lefkovitz frowned.

"What's the downer now?" Jake said, afraid that it would be the same as always—that his father wouldn't even try to see all the ways he had changed.

Jake said, "Dad, I've got good instincts. I know how to listen to them now. Hey, I come from great genes. Just give me a chance."

Dr. Lefkovitz turned away from him and went to a crude control board radiating electric cables, and threw a switch. Two hundred feet above the camp, the jungle canopy lit up with long strings of naked lightbulbs lining each of the dozens of aerial walkways and rope bridges that spread out from a high central platform like the support spokes of a circus tent. A gasoline truck motor, reclaimed from an abandoned gold-mining operation, chugged away driving a crude generator at the edge of the river.

"The only way you can help around here is to keep out of our way."

"Okay, Dad," Jake said. He'd long ago learned it was easier to yes his father than argue. He'd always soften after a while, and usually forget anything harsh that he'd said. "I will," Jake went on. "I'll stay on the ground. I'll wash laundry. Anything. I don't care. I'll become the best worker you've got. You'll be glad I came." Jake's gaze was fixed skyward on the dangling walkways and lights, to the high-wire glitter show—an adventure he knew he had no intention of missing.

The jungle became a wall of night by the time Jake had stowed his things. The camp itself was still ablaze from the garlands of lightbulbs. Jake's bed, in the largest hut, was on the other side of the room from his father's. They were separated by a towering rack of formaldehyde jars brimming with vampire bat specimens. Dozens of small mouths were agape and distorted. A sky of small black, dead eyes appeared to stare down at him. Jake hated the way scientists killed hundreds, if not thousands, of creatures just to add them to their collection. He never forgot an experiment one of his father's colleagues had done once on mice. He put electrodes into the brains of living mice, and then decapitated the mice to check on how their nervous systems worked. Jake had nightmares for months when he'd heard about that project.

There came the sound from a bamboo flute, loud and shrill, and Dr. Lefkovitz's voice: "Hey, Jake—get out here for dinner."

"Coming," Jake called back.

Outside, his father, Hanuma and the dozen or so Indian workers from the camp sat cross-legged on mats that covered the ground of the communal circle.

"We start our work up in the canopy after dinner," his father said.

"I want to go up with you," Jake said, sitting down next to his father.

"It's too dangerous—I don't want you up there."

"I . . ." Jake started, but a bowl of roast pig and plump, moist bark larvae was placed in front of him. Jake knew the thick white worms were a delicacy throughout the Amazon. He also knew the men were watching him, waiting to see what he'd do.

"Ummm," he said, picking out one of the crispiest larvae, putting it in his mouth, and chewing on it like a caramel.

Hanuma and the workers smiled.

"Magyar is our cook," Hanuma said. "He trapped and cooked the fresh boar to celebrate your arrival."

Jake looked at the small Indian across from him who was smiling and nodding his head.

"Thank you, Magyar," Jake said. He grabbed a piece of the wild pig and tasted it. There were softer, moist clumps clinging to it. Magyar spoke excitedly as Jake realized how tasty the clumps were.

"He wants you to know the boar was stuffed and wrapped with masticated water snake."

"He's spoiling me," Jake said.

Hanuma laughed loudly.

"Dad, I want you to see this gadget I made." Jake opened his equipment box and took out a jerry-rigged power belt with a cluster of wires that looked like the kind used to hook up a VCR. He tightened the belt around his waist, reached back into the box, and hooked up a screen and circuit board he'd adapted from an old video game.

"I can't give it any time now," his father said.

"Maybe tonight after work. I remember last year's science fair project. You made that electronic kitty litter box—the one where the top lifted when anything crossed in front of an electric eye. And it did something when the lid closed."

"Gave a spray of perfume."

"Yes. It almost scared our cat to death."

"Hey, I was only fooling around," Jake said. "This year I did something serious on bat flight and communication."

"We'll see," his father said. He brushed flecks of charred meat from his lap, and stood up. The men got to their feet and headed for the rope ladders. Dangari and Muras sat in the two-man sling elevator. It looked like a parachute harness with a swing seat. They threw a switch to engage the power shaft that had been geared to the truck engine. The sling jerked upward, lifting the men quickly to the central canopy platform.

"Pops, I want to go up," Jake said.

His father frowned again.

Hanuma spoke up. "The riverwalk of the canopy needs repairing. Can you tie knots?" he asked Jake.

"I'm the best knot-tying expert in the world," Jake answered quickly. "I was an Eagle Scout."

Dr. Lefkovitz stared at Hanuma a moment, then smiled. "All right," he told Jake. "You can help reinforce the walkways. Hanuma will show you how to use the vines. The rest of us will be collecting specimens on the north walkway tonight."

The empty sling was sent back down. Dr. Lefkovitz and one of the other workers got into it and went up.

"We'll be next," Hanuma said.

"I could climb," Jake said. "I only fell twice in gym class—that's because it was a single rope and I had to climb using my hands only."

"This canopy is two hundred feet high—it's not your gym ceiling," Hanuma said. "You would fall only once here."

4 • THE CANOPY

While Dr. Lefkovitz and Magyar traveled up to the canopy, Jake shook out a shoulder pouch he'd packed and put his echolocation device into it. The sling arrived back down, and Jake sat in it with Hanuma. Jake gasped as the seat jerked up into the air like the harness of a rising parachute.

"Hey, this *is* high," Jake said, as they were lifted quickly to the canopy platform. The central platform itself was an octagonal scaffold that encircled the top of the tallest mahogany tree. His father and the other workers had already started out along the rope bridges and slatted track of the north walkway.

Hanuma pointed to a walkway to the left that appeared to end at a wall of thick vines and foliation. "That is the riverwalk," Hanuma said. He led Jake to a spot high above the bank of the river. "Your father started collecting here three months ago when we arrived, but the canopy was too thick above the river. Unyielding. It is a barrier because the mist of the river rises and feeds the jungle above it more than any other area."

Jake set his shoulder pouch down on the walkway. "So where do I tie knots?"

Hanuma sat down cross-legged, and grabbed a thin, strong vine from the edge of the walkway. He took the machete hanging from his waist and sliced the vine into lengths as long as his arm.

"You tie the slats together," Hanuma said. "We use bow knots. Do you know bow knots?"

"Sure," Jake said. "Bow knots were my specialty when I was an Eagle."

"Good," Hanuma said, smiling. "Up here it is excellent to be an eagle."

Jake watched Hanuma make the first tie. The old vine-ties were frayed, rotting. Hanuma placed the new vine over the old, and tied the knots so that one of the slats of the walkway was firmly attached to the next.

"Like *that*," Hanuma said.

"Right," Jake said.

Jake took off his shoulder pouch and sat down across from Hanuma, then selected a piece of fresh cut vine and bound together the pair of slats in front of him. With his father and the other men gone, he could hear the sounds of insects and monkeys in the canopy. One area had been hacked away enough so Jake could glimpse the river flowing below.

Hanuma gave Jake his machete. "Cut back the overgrowth, but don't sever the rope railings," he said. "Be careful."

Jake swung the machete, and the vines and young branches gave way bit by bit. Once they had worked their way farther out over the river itself, Jake knew that if the fall to the river didn't kill him, the piranha would.

"What do you think happened to the two missing workers?" Jake asked. "I mean, what do you *really* think?"

"No one knows," Hanuma said. "They were working here on the riverwalk the night they disappeared. That was almost two weeks ago. They finished with the rest of us, and went down."

Jake looked more carefully at the wall of jungle

that lay ahead on the riverwalk. A coolness rose up from the river far below. "How do you know for sure that they didn't run away?"

"We searched around the camp. There were no footprints, no signs that anyone had left the camp in any direction."

"Maybe they left on the river."

Hanuma took his machete back to cut several more strips of tough vine. "No pirogues were missing. They couldn't have swum very far because of the piranha."

Jake tied another set of the planks together.

"Did anyone see them climb down or use the sling?"

"No."

Jake winked at Hanuma. "I thought you were supposed to be clairvoyant? That you could feel things. See things that were happening elsewhere?"

"I don't have good feelings about the disappearance of these men, but I've chosen to hope and pray to the Great Spirit they are still alive."

"Well, I've been thinking about them, too," Jake said, "Ever since Dad called and told us. I've been having bad dreams. Usually, it's because I eat too much popcorn before going to bed. But, I've had these dreams about the men, and bats coming after me—and about a dozen other horrible Amazon bugs and critters I've read about. Since I was in the third grade, I've had a recurring dream that one day I'll be devoured alive.

"There was always something I was afraid of. Once, for school, I researched all the documented shark attacks in the world since recorded history. I had nightmares about sharks for years," Jake said. He looked around at the shadows in the canopy. "Did you ever think that maybe the missing men were still up here in the canopy? Did you ever consider that?"

Hanuma glanced uneasily toward the barrier of vines and branches. "The men had been ordered to clear the riverwalk," he said.

Jake took the machete back and chopped carefully at the next cluster of the green wall.

"If a jaguar had taken them, we would have heard screams. A jungle cat would silence only one man at a time," Hanuma said.

"I know jaguars bite the throat and cut off your breathing," Jake said.

"Yes, that is the way they kill. They are merciful—they do not eat a man alive."

Jake reached into his shoulder pouch and pulled out his electronic device. He flicked a switch and his gadget made a high pulsing noise.

Blip . . . Blip . . .

"This is Gizmo," Jake explained to Hanuma. "That's what I call it."

"Gizmo?"

"Yep."

"What does Gizmo *do*?"

"A couple of things," Jake said. "I built the device keeping in mind that bats make all kinds of noises, both audible and ultrasonic. The audible 'blip' sounds Gizmo makes travel out and bounce off objects, like tree trunks and stones. Whatever. Different things have different densities and don't reflect sound waves the same." He set Gizmo's small glowing video screen on his lap. "The sounds come back and we see a 'picture.' Pictures of things in the jungle."

"You can see *through* the jungle?"

Jake explained that Gizmo could "see" easily for a hundred feet or so. He had built a volume dial into Gizmo so he could pump up the sound and make the signals reach up to several hundred feet into the night or jungle. Bats usually send out high frequency sounds and can see in the dark. Some use audible vocalizations like Gizmo's in communication—between mothers and their young, among roost mates, and, in some species of bats, as alarm cries. The echoes let them see shapes. Gizmo's picture made everything black and white, more like an X ray or the image on an oscilloscope screen.

"So what will you do with Gizmo?" Hanuma asked.

"I'm not sure yet," Jake replied. "Can you show me where the men were working before they disappeared?"

"There."

Jake aimed the directional disc of the device so it pointed straight at the spot Hanuma was indicating.

Blip . . .

The sounds went out and were reflected back. Images danced on the small game screen. "You can see motion on this thing," Jake said. "I mean, it's hard to see the definite shape of anything—but we'll be able to look pretty deep into the canopy. You've got to train your eye." Jake pointed out a configuration on the screen. "See, that's a big tree trunk."

"Your father wouldn't like you playing up here," Hanuma said.

"Hey, this isn't play. I mean, I *won* the whole school science fair with Gizmo." A thin, twisting image moved in the lower section of the screen. Jake felt a flush of apprehension, then recognized what it was. "See, that's a snake in the canopy."

Hanuma watched the image for a moment. "Yes. There are many small tree pythons here," Hanuma said. "They are harmless, much smaller than the ordinary pythons that can crush you to death. They're not poisonous. We don't need Gizmo to tell us this."

"Maybe your men *accidentally* fell into the river," Jake said. "They could have been out on a branch, and it broke off."

"They didn't cut far enough into the overgrowth to be above the river. They would have fallen onto the bank."

Jake put the strap of his apparatus around his neck, and stood slowly. He turned up the amplitude of the blips. Hanuma stood and looked over his shoulder.

"What is this?" Hanuma asked, pointing to a dark shape in the middle of the screen.

Jake checked it and said, "Maybe a clump of vines."

"Why is it moving?"

"The wind," Jake said, but a spray of goose bumps rose on the back of his neck. "It looks like it could be something that's alive, but it's too big. Maybe sap flowing from a hollow trunk."

Jake used the machete and hacked deeper. With each slash, clumps of vines and branches fell away. They were farther from the lighted stretch of the riverwalk.

"We should come back with floodlights or a Coleman lamp," Jake said hesitantly.

Hanuma watched the image of the undulating object come into focus. Near the base of it there were twisted shapes.

"Hey," Jake said. "It could be just a rotting branch or some kind of hive or bark maggots. . . ."

With another powerful slash of the machete, a drape of vines dropped onto the abandoned walkway. Jake reflexively kicked the clump out of the way. In front of him was a shining bulk that swelled as high as the thick rope railings. The dim light spill rendered the mass a sort of shroud.

"There are bones," Hanuma said.

Jake gave the machete back to Hanuma, picked up a broken branch, and prodded at the center of the form. Now he could see that whatever it was, it was covered with hundreds of tiny black moving *wings.*

5 • ATTACK

"It's just bats," Jake said. "A colony of little vampire bats. *Desmodus rotundus.*" Jake had read about them and seen pictures of this species of Amazon bat.

"It is something more," Hanuma said.

Using the branch, Jake gritted his teeth as he prodded deeper into the colony. The bats began to make high-pitched sounds, peel away from the mound, and take to the air. They flapped away into a labyrinth of holes that had been ripped out of the underbelly of the canopy. Those bats that stayed on the heap were drinking, their tongues frantically lapping at an oozing fluid.

Hanuma said, "They're drinking blood."

Jake yelled. He wanted to see what dead prey was beneath them. He thought it could be a large blue heron or jungle vulture, a favorite feast for vampires. A bird could have gotten sick in the tree, and the vampires overwhelmed it.

But the clump was bigger. Larger and tangled.

Hanuma stepped away from the light.

They saw the oozing mass clearly now. Protruding from the top of the bloody clump were the ghastly remains of a pair of human heads, their cheeks and necks and black hair twisted and fused. Fragments of white skull glistened, and strips of light shot into holes where once there had been eyes and brains. Desiccated feet and hands and more cracked and broken bone appeared to hold the clump up, to support it like the base of a blood-soaked sculpture. The mutilated cadavers of two men, each with a shattered jaw and a mouth frozen open in a death scream.

Jake's eyes burned and his nostrils flared from the sickening stench. "No little bats did all this," he said, his voice breaking. But Hanuma had already turned and was heading back on the riverwalk.

There was another sound now: *Bleep . . . bleep . . .*

It was different from the blips Gizmo

generated for its searching sonar. Jake remembered turning the blip generator off. Now Gizmo was up picking the sounds of something approaching.

Coming fast.

"Hanuma," he called. "Wait."

Hanuma kept moving. "I'll get your father. . . ."

Jake realized he'd left Gizmo's receiver on. The *bleeps* were coming closer, louder. He could hear a pulsing screech. A high pitch, as from a large bird or animal—something big crashing through the canopy. Tearing through vines and jungle.

Wings flapping.

The lights of the river ramp went out, and there was only the glowing spill from the central platform. Jake saw the image on the screen now. Something bulky, moving fast. It was thirty to forty feet to the left, tearing through the canopy and the open pockets of its underbelly. The river was two hundred feet below.

The imaged creature was past him now.

"Watch out, Hanuma," Jake called. "It's heading toward you!"

Hanuma heard Jake's cries. All he could think of was getting to Dr. Lefkovitz. Dr. Lefkovitz would know what to do. He'd know what had killed the men. What kind of evil. Hanuma felt overwhelmed by a malevolence that made his skin hot and wet. The badness of the place. A profanity. He felt the cries of the men. An evil hung in the air, brushed against him like the hanging vines and creepers on the sides of the riverwalk. Branches scraped his arms, and caught in his long gray hair as he ran toward the light.

Hanuma heard the hunting creature, too. The large thing racing, flapping its way through the canopy. It sounded as though it were a large puma or jaguar rapidly closing the distance between them. Bad thing. Dangerous thing. He believed he could hear spirits crying out: *Don't let it get you. Don't—*

The eruption came from the canopy wall on his left. Hanuma saw a giant bat hurl itself out at him like a winged panther. He glimpsed its claws and leathery, muscled arms. Its wings opened like a cloak of skin and its abdomen was swollen and hairy like that of a ugly, colossal moth. The creature hit into him as his brain registered clearly the enormous, wide head with large green eyes set above a squashed snout.

The impact of the giant bat knocked Hanuma down. He tried to reach for his machete, but the weapon tumbled across the walkway and over the edge. Claws locked on his shoulders like vises. Hanuma was ashamed of his scream—a scream like that of an old woman. He shrieked again, as the monstrous bat drove its two long fangs deep into his neck, the honed, pointed teeth plunging into Hanuma's spine. He trembled as his blood burst out onto the walkway in front of him.

Jake was stunned when the creature exploded from the canopy. He saw it seize Hanuma, biting and clawing at him viciously. The walkway shook violently, and Jake had to grab for the rope railing to stop from falling over the side and down into the river.

Whatever the beast was, Jake saw it pulling Hanuma fast toward the central platform—Hanuma's limp body sliding quickly away. Jake steadied himself and started after Hanuma and the monster. The creature was dragging the old man by the neck, half carrying him over the planks, using its wing tips like crutches—like the bats in Jake's nightmare! The giant bat was trying to haul Hanuma off into the canopy. Into the air.

"Help! Help!" Jake called out, hoping his father would hear.

He gained ground. A hundred thoughts shot

through Jake's mind at once. He thought of the power pack around his waist. He thought of Gizmo, and of just throwing himself on the creature. He'd try to stamp on its wings and make it break its grip on Hanuma.

Jake was shouting at the thing now, shouting at it as if it were a bad dog: "Drop him! You drop him! You let him loose!"

6 • SCREAMS

Dr. Lefkovitz and the men heard Hanuma and the cries for help. The old shaman's screams were heart-stopping, Jake's shouts chilling. Several of the men were harvesting bat specimens from traps along a rope bridge. There was no way they could make it back quickly onto the slatted stretch of the north walkway.

Along with Dangari and Muras, Dr. Lefkovitz reacted as if he'd heard a bomb go off. The frightened men turned back, moving as fast as they dared on the aerial walkway.

Jake—his father thought. *What if he's fallen! What if he or Hanuma has fallen!*

Near the central platform, the north walkway

angled and ran parallel to the riverwalk. Dr. Lefkovitz first saw Hanuma across the gulf between the cat-walks. His body was sliding as if by magic, a limp doll nearly airborne, grasped in the jaws of darkness.

Dr. Lefkovitz gasped. "Oh, my God."

Closer, he saw the shape of the shadowy thing, retreating with its spoils. The lights on the riverwalk were out. Hanuma's body was being carried head-first now, his face raised so that his eyes stared up into the snarling mouth of the beast.

Dangari and Muras slowed, trembled. Dr. Lefkovitz saw them holding back.

"Come on!" he ordered.

Suddenly, Jake burst from the shadows of the riverwalk, racing to save Hanuma. Jake was acting on instinct now. He had turned up the volume on Gizmo. Its speakers were blaring. Earsplitting. *Blip . . . Blipblipblipblip . . .*

The pitch from the device was painful, excruci-ating, and the bat creature was outraged by it. It halted and shrieked on the approach to the center platform. The massive bat looked around, saw the other, stronger men stampeding toward it, the shout-ing men on the north walkway crossing over.

Jake tore off the power belt and grasped one end

of it as if it were a length of heavy chain. The creature had dragged Hanuma into deeper shadows. It was a murky shape now, with a single splash of light bouncing off its glistening, snouted head.

The bat thrust its wings violently forward as Jake swung the power belt in a high arc. Its weight of lead casings and batteries hit the creature on the skull. The bat let out a shriek, and its clawed legs flew out toward Jake. It snorted wildly, a stinking, vile mucous flying from its nostrils. Jake swung the belt again. And again.

His father, Dangari, and Muras were racing across the central platform. The bat had withdrawn its blood-covered fangs from Hanuma's neck and dropped him. The old man was still conscious, moaning on the walkway, as the bat turned. Suddenly, with a final shriek, the bat propelled itself over the side and plummeted toward the jungle floor.

Jake sunk to his knees and cradled Hanuma until the others reached him. Dangari and Muras helped tend to the wounded shaman. Dr. Lefkovitz was riveted at the railing. He saw the falling monster spread its wings and go into a glide. It circled quickly, terrifyingly, then headed out toward the river and the jungle night.

It was a while before Jake and his father descended in the sling. They waited below as Dangari and Muras brought Hanuma down. Dr. Lefkovitz made the old man as comfortable as possible on a cot of woven hemp in the main hut.

"You're going downstream to the missionary village," Dr. Lefkovitz told the barely conscious Hanuma. "Jake told me what happened. We saw the creature."

"I'm sorry . . . very sorry," Hanuma said, gasping. He struggled to hold up his head.

Jake got a pair of his jeans and a T-shirt. He rolled them up and placed them under Hanuma's head for a pillow. Dr. Lefkovitz carefully injected an anti-rabies vaccine into the folds of Hanuma's stomach, and a local anesthetic into the periphery of the wounds at the back of his neck. He cleaned and cauterized the punctures and lacerations from the bite and attack. "You'll need an intravenous drip to prevent you from going into shock. You save your energy—rest. Everything will be okay," Dr. Lefkovitz said gently.

Hanuma closed his eyes. He began to breathe deeply. His body was still trembling. Dangari draped

Hanuma's old and frayed shaman's robe about him to comfort him, to wrap him in the spirit and power and tribal dreams it still held for Hanuma.

"What will happen at the missionary camp?" Jake asked.

"Their radio is powerful enough to reach the Brazilian Army installation at Jacaranda," his father said. "They'll send a medic in a helicopter and airlift him to Manaus."

Jake took a bottle of alcohol from the supply stock next to the jars of formaldehyde filled with the bat specimens. He dabbed at his own scrapes and bruises. His father hesitated, then took over helping to clean the cuts for him. For a moment, Jake felt his father was going to praise him for saving Hanuma on the riverwalk.

"You shouldn't have come," his father said instead. His voice was cold, covering any real emotion, as usual. "You don't understand the jungle. You don't know what you're dealing with here."

"Dad, I . . ."

His father didn't let him speak. "You were way out of line bringing your little electronic game up to the canopy. . . ."

"It's not a game."

"Now you know why I never want you with me. . . ."

Jake let his father go on. *Why can't you see me, Dad?* Jake felt like shouting. *Why can't you really see me?*

7 • METAMORPHOSIS

Magyar and three of the other men brought down the remains of the two dead workers. Dr. Lefkovitz left the hut to examine what was left of the twisted and hollowed bodies. Jake stayed with Hanuma to make certain the drip needle didn't slip out of the wrist vein and bloat the arm. He himself was still shaken from the confrontation with the huge bat. He needed to talk alone with his father. It seemed to him there were a lot of questions that needed to be asked, and decisions to be made.

Sorgno, one of the younger workers, came in to check on Hanuma. Jake asked Sorgno to stay with the old man while he went out by the campfire and waited until he could get his father aside. Several of the other workers had already placed thick logs and chunks of peat on the campfires so they blazed to help ward off the chill and the terror.

"Will Hanuma be all right?" Jake whispered to his father. "The bite was deep. That thing's fangs were like knives. What kind of creature was it?"

"I've never seen nor heard of any species of bat that large or ferocious," his father said. "Even in Indonesia the Megachiroptera don't get half that big. The biggest bat known is a fruit bat." His father's voice became strangely hollow, a tone Jake knew from long experience meant that his father was filtering his words, too carefully choosing what he wanted to say.

"You're not telling me something," Jake said.

His father dropped his gaze to the ground. Jake new that look, too—another familiar, evasive maneuver. "Son, the Amazon is as big and unexplored as the depths of the ocean. There could be anything down here. . . ."

"Dad, what don't you want me to know?"

Dr. Lefkovitz turned to look at the roaring fires. "We had a warning, I suppose. About the bat, perhaps. The first month the expedition had settled here, Hanuma and I took a pirogue and went upriver about a dozen miles to a small village—a *malorca* of Kano Indians—true primitives and known in past times to be headhunters. As we approached the village's mud beach, there were thirty or forty of the Kanos who had come down to the bank. Naked men with straw woven into their hair. Women with moonstone necklaces holding children. Children playing tag in the mud."

"What happened?" Jake asked.

His father turned back to look Jake in the eye. "Closer, I noticed several of the villagers throwing what looked like large chunks of meat and bone into the water. All around the 'meat,' the river boiled with the flash of silver fish. I insisted we stop. I asked Hanuma why the Kanos were feeding the piranha. Hanuma said we should keep going—that it would be dangerous to stop—but I wanted to know what was going on.

"Hanuma and I let the boat drift into the shallows, but we held our paddles ready. We had to circle around the massive school of feeding piranha. Some of the fish were a foot—a foot and a half!— long. Larger than any piranha I'd ever seen. The fish hurled themselves at the food, sinking their teeth deep, then shaking their bodies ferociously until a shred of the meat tore loose. I saw what they were being fed: pieces of human bodies."

Jake's tongue thickened. His shirt was damp, too tight about his chest.

His father went on. "The villagers were tossing into the river parts of what seemed to have once been a man and a woman—perhaps a couple of children, too," his father continued. "Hands and feet that had been hacked off—the remains of a savage slaughtering."

Jake fought the sickening feeling that was swelling in his stomach. "Who killed them?"

"That's what I wanted to know. Hanuma called to the villagers. A shaman came forward and spoke in a language Hanuma understood. 'The slaughtered men and women were a family,' Hanuma translated for me. 'The village had to kill them because the family was about to turn into beasts.'"

"What was the shaman talking about?" Jake asked.

"Hanuma had another exchange, then tried to explain to me that the shaman believed that, in this village, every few years, some people change into terrible winged creatures. Monsters that begin to kill and devour the other villagers. They hang their victims high in the jungle. Demons. Phantoms. The slaughtered family had begun its metamorphosis."

"You and Hanuma didn't believe that, did you?" Jake asked.

"No," his father said. " *'Get us out of here,'* I told Hanuma. Together, we paddled back out, straight through the water boiling with the feeding piranha. Hanuma kept talking to the tribe's shaman. Smiling. Laughing. I knew Hanuma was calming the tribe. Assuring the shaman and the villagers that we were leaving in peace. . . ."

"Do you think the winged monster could have been this big bat?" Jake asked. "That this bat has been feeding on the village and they explained it with this metamorphosis—this crazy belief that people in the village could turn into monsters? I mean, that's nuts."

"Yes," his father said. "But I should have listened more carefully. Asked more questions. I think they have seen this bat."

"Maybe it's a creature that has lived here all along—since time began—and it doesn't happen to like a lot of people invading its territory. You—the expedition—you're the real invaders around here, aren't you? I read a lot before deciding to come down here, Dad. The Indians have been here for twenty thousand years and everything went just fine. They took care of the jungle and the jungle took care of them."

"That's got nothing to do with that bat. . . ."

"It could," Jake said. "I mean, you couldn't blame the jungle if it started fighting back." He remembered Hanuma. "Hey, that bat could have given Hanuma rabies, right?"

"If it was infected, the virus would be in its spittle. In its bite."

"Its saliva was in Hanuma's wounds," Jake said. "It was in his neck."

"And upper spine," his father added. "If the bite were on Hanuma's hands or legs, he might have as much as three to six weeks before the symptoms of rabies—the madness—could begin. Once the virus reaches the brain, there's no cure. The rabies virus feeds on the brain cells and drives its victim insane. Hydrophobia. Fear of water. A horror of *everything*—in its final stages. It is the most terrifying death imaginable—but, even if Hanuma is infected, he's got a good chance of getting through this if we get him downstream tonight. I started his rabies shots, but he's going to require a series of them over several days. The Fathers at the village will continue the injections until the helicopter can get him to the hospital in Manaus."

Dangari and Muras interrupted. They took Dr. Lefkovitz aside, whispering for his ears only. When he came back to Jake, his father said, "They're ready to put Hanuma in the pirogue."

"Dad, you've been here for months. You've got enough dead bats to choke a hippo. Besides, the whole place is going to flood any week now. How many more flying rats do you have to knock off?"

The sound of men chanting drifted to them from the edge of the camp. The workers were standing around the open grave they'd dug for the dead men. Dangari came over and asked Dr. Lefkovitz to say a few words. Together they walked to the grave.

Muras made room for Jake to stand next to him as his father spoke in a prayerful tone: "They were two loyal and fine friends—members of our research team. They were good family men and spoke often about their children. I will see that the monies they earned will reach their families. The museum sponsoring the expedition will provide extra funds. We will do as much as we can. . . ."

The grave was deep, moist, with sides that

glistened in the moonlight. Jake lifted his eyes from the shadowy, twisted cadavers lying at the bottom of the grave, and glanced around the circle of the men. He saw the worker he'd left with Hanuma.

If that guy's here, then who's with Hanuma? Jake thought with alarm. He counted heads. Everyone was standing around the grave except Hanuma. *Did you leave Hanuma alone?* Jake wanted to shout.

Jake turned as a cry shattered the night. Hanuma was standing in front of the blazing fire—the center fire roaring from extra logs and branches piled on to keep the creature away. The old man's hands clawed up toward the sky, as if he were trying to strangle a phantom. *"Ranca di!"* he screamed. *"Gara di ranca!"*

Several of the men at the grave cried out as Hanuma walked forward *into* the fire, wailing the words over and over.

"Gara di ranca!"

Dangari raced toward him. He and Muras reached him as the hem of his robe caught fire. He collapsed with a final scream.

The men tore the burning robe off Hanuma. Magyar scooped water from the drinking trough and spilled it on Hanuma's legs. They lay him down. Dr. Lefkovitz was at his side, kneeling, checking

Hanuma's feet and ankles. His feet were calloused, black with charcoal. The other men surrounded them now, and Dr. Lefkovitz heard the fear in their stammering.

"He isn't burned," Dr. Lefkovitz said, finally. "A little singed hair on his legs, but he's fine."

Dangari translated the English for those of the men who didn't understand.

"We should leave now for the village," Muras said.

Dr. Lefkovitz nodded.

Dangari and Muras covered Hanuma's naked body with a sheet and carried him to the beached pirogue they had prepared. They lay the old man down gently on a bed of crushed palm and young ferns arranged in the dugout and lifted the pirogue into the shallows. Muras took the bow seat, Dangari the stern. Workers waded into the water and guided the pirogue until it was clear of the shallows. The rapid central flow of the river caught the dugout. Dangari and Muras grasped their paddles and began deep, rhythmic strokes into the dark water.

8 • THE FALLS

Jake waved a solemn farewell with the others on the bank as the pirogue moved off swiftly downstream through the mist and moonlight. He asked his father, "Did you give them a gun?"

"We have no guns," his father said.

"That's not too smart, is it?"

"It's the law here, enforced by tribal decree. We are guests here for research. Spears. Traps. Poison darts and blow guns are used to slay animals for food. The Murdaruci can hit a parrot a hundred feet high the trees."

Jake felt nauseous, but his own shivering had stopped. He was frightened about Hanuma's jouney. He knew that the trip downstream to the missionary village wouldn't be long. He remembered the trip upstream very well, and estimated the pirogue would reach Dark Angel Falls in less than an hour.

"There are two other smaller falls between Dark Angel and the missionary camp," his father said.

Jake recalled them and knew those wouldn't be a problem. What he worried about was how difficult it would be for Dangari and Muras to carry Hanuma and the dugout down the steep, rocky bank and past the violent whirlpools at the base of the tremendous drop of Dark Angel Falls.

The men returned to the grave. The sound of shovels thrusting into the dirt, and the thud as each scoop fell, was like the ticking of a clock. Jake wanted to put his hands over his ears.

"What is *'Gara di ranca'*?" Jake asked Magyar. "What was Hanuma saying?"

"It is Murdaruci,'" Magyar said. "Hanuma was furious at the sky and the Great Spirit. He had fever. A sickness in his head. I'm certain that he didn't know what he was saying. It was a question."

"What?"

"Hanuma asked the Great Spirit why it had sent us doom."

★ ★ ★

55

Dangari worried as the mist of the river became as blinding as fog. He and Muras paddled quietly, doing nothing to mute or sully the sounds of the rushing water. They knew the pure sounds of the river, and, if they listened carefully, they could navigate a pirogue on it blindfolded. They would hear the white water and falls in plenty of time to find a favorite safe pool or backwater near the bank.

There was a break in the mist and they saw a flight of pink ibis fly across the front of the bow and up into the moonlight. White-collared marabou storks strutted along a marshy bank. Muras caught a glimpse of a jaguar sitting high in a rubber tree.

Soon, the blinding mist returned and closed down upon them like a white ceiling. Dangari leaned forward and placed a cool hand on Hanuma's brow. The old, thin shaman looked like he was sleeping. His waist-long hair fanned out at his sides and stirred in the river wind.

"We'll soon be at the village," Dangari whispered in Murdaruci. Soothing. Wanting the old man to know he was with his good and trusted friends. His favorite workers . . .

Hanuma's eyes opened. He moved his lips, but no words could be heard.

"You rest," Muras said. "The Fathers will be happy to see you."

Hanuma smiled. He listened to the sound of wavelets slapping at the hull. The pirogue rocked gently with each plunge of a paddle. He stared up at the billowing whiteness above him, felt as if he could reach up his hand and touch it like a ceiling. He heard the sounds of the ibis and jumping fish, the movement of a large alligator across the muddy bank. Hanuma wanted to believe the journey would go well. He heard the rush of the water against the rocks. Without raising his head, he knew exactly where they were on the river.

"We will be at Dark Angel soon," Dangari said.

Hanuma nodded. He thought about sleeping until then. He turned his head to the side and smelled the freshness of the palm and fern bedding beneath him. He wouldn't think about the bat. The creature. He was too weak for that. He decided to believe he was in a swing. Yes, that was it. The dugout was a hammock—like the one his father had once made for him out of twisted vines and the bark of a kapock tree.

But there came another sound.

Dangari heard it first. His hearing was always the

best. At first, he believed it was a large stork or night heron taking flight upstream. It was a flapping of wings. Large wings. Something large flying toward them.

The flapping noise grew louder. Whatever it was, it was just above them now. Something flying, hidden by the mist.

Something following them.

9 • EFFIGIES

J ake knew Hanuma's outburst had terrorized the workers. From time to time, he had seen frightened people at accident scenes in Manhattan. Firemen as they arrived at a tenement that was a flaming inferno. Victims strewn on the sidewalk of Fifth Avenue after a bus jumped the curb and plowed into a crowd of Christmas shoppers. Frightened men and women had a look in their eyes. Time seemed to stand still, and sometimes they babbled nearly incoherently. They walked in circles and blessed themselves and wept.

The Indians tonight moved quickly to set several more camp fires about the grounds and shouted at the night to try to keep the monstrous creature away. The fires blazed, fueled by the logs and kindling that had been intended to last at least three more weeks or until the floods hit.

Dr. Lefkovitz didn't try to stop the men from their fire building. He knew it was what any jungle villagers would do if a man-eater was on the prowl.

With Dangari and Muras transporting Hanuma downstream, only Magyar had enough English to communicate clearly what was happening. Several of the men had taken hammers and what remained of the two by fours brought up from Manaus. Others tore apart a lean-to and began to make a dozen or so of what appeared to be large crosses.

"What are they doing?" Jake asked his father.

"Making effigies," his father said.

The workers began to gather bundles of yellow reeds and young bamboo from the bank, and tie them onto the wooden structures so they appeared to have arms and legs and heads. The figures took shape and, when held upright, stood five and six feet tall.

"It's really weird," Jake said. "Shouldn't they be doing something else?"

"It'd be like telling Kansas farmers they can't have scarecrows," his father said. "They think the effigies will fool the bat like they can trick a jaguar. I've seen tribes do it in India and Africa, too. Scarecrows to fool man-eaters—rogue lions and tigers—in thinking that there are many more warriors than there really are. In the South Indian swamps, the families make effigies and wear masks on the back of their heads."

"Why the *back* of their heads?"

"Most big cats don't attack from the front. They don't attack if you're looking at them. The masks on the back of the natives' heads are a trick that works for a while, but sometimes the animals catch on. They get so they can tell—perhaps smell!—which are the real faces and real people. Then the masks don't work any more."

The workers used hammers and an ax handle to drive the base of the life-size effigies into the soft ground. Jake found the sight of the scarecrows standing around the camp really scary. "Why don't we just get out of here?" Jake said.

"There are some very important things I need to do before I can leave," his father said. "I can arrange for a couple of the workers to take you downstream in the morning. These men aren't experienced enough to be on the river at night."

"What are you talking about?" Jake said. "I'm not leaving without you. And I've got Gizmo. You've got to see what Gizmo can do."

For a moment, Jake thought his father could see how he'd changed. "I could use every man," his father said, finally, "but it's best if you go."

"Hey, you *need* me."

His father dropped his gaze. "We'll talk about this later. Now I need to talk to the men. It'd be better if you wait in the hut. The men would feel strange with you there."

"Oh, yeah," Jake said. "I forgot, I'm not a member of the team."

Jake spun on his heel and marched himself into the hut, slapping closed its canvas door flap so it made a *whaaack*. He heard his father calling Magyar to gather the men around the central campfire. Jake threw himself down on his cot, and clasped his hands around the back of his neck. He stared at the yellowing, thatched ceiling. Why does the bat eat brains, he wondered. What kind of creature feasts on the human mind?

Dangari was thankful the sound of the wings had gone away. It had been something above them for a few minutes—something hidden in the thick night fog, and then had moved on.

"We should start to head for shore," Dangari said to Muras.

"Yes," Muras said.

The river was narrowing before the falls, and the flow was faster. Dangari was thankful when they passed around a final turn and there was a break in the mist and river fog. Moonlight lit the way clear to the falls. There was ample time to rudder the boat toward the largest backwater pool on the left bank. It was as they guided the boat toward the haven that they saw a dark shape hanging from the gnarled trunk of a grandiflora tree.

Dangari tried not to sound frightened. "We must head for the other shore."

"Yes," Muras agreed.

Hanuma stirred from his sleep. He had somehow heard fear creep into his friend's voices. He began to send his thoughts skyward to ask the Great Spirit to protect them. *Get us to the village safely*, Hanuma prayed. *If I have ever been a kind and good shaman, let us pass the Dark Angel . . . let us pass. . . .*

His body started to tremble again. He tried to raise his head, but he was too weak.

Dangari and Muras turned the boat. The falls were still far enough away for them to make it to the right bank of thick, lush jungle. Even without a backwater pool or cover, they could grasp the dense overhang of mogno branches and berry vines, and stop the boat.

The bat waited until the pirogue was in the middle of the river before it dropped away from the tree trunk and took to the air. Dangari saw it gliding toward them, its immense, shining wings strangely beautiful in the moonlight.

"Faster," Dangari told Muras.

Muras dug his paddle harder and deeper into the water. The current was treacherous now. It would take all their strength to reach the bank before the eddies and white water would totally seize the boat.

Dangari needed to keep his focus on plunging his paddle with more power. Deeper still. He couldn't think about the flapping sound. The sound of the wings behind him came closer. He felt a shadow pass between him and the moon.

Muras, too, cut his paddle into the water with more strength and speed than he'd thought possible. Panic began to creep into his stomach, and a stench of rotting carrion descended and burned in his nostrils. The fluttering of wings became drowned out by the roar of the falls. Dangari leaned forward as he stabbed the water with his paddle. There was still a chance, he thought. As long as the creature didn't attack. As long as they could keep the boat lunging forward toward the land.

Just make it to the overhang.

They would be safe.

Abruptly, the blackness swooped down. That was all Dangari could see at first: a huge, rippling blackness in front of him. He felt the pirogue shudder and rock as the dark thing struck the boat. Muras was immediately spilled into the turbulent water. There was no time for words. Or cries for help. Muras tried to swim out of the current which took hold of him with the force of a whirlpool.

Dangari struck fiercely at the water with his paddle. Alone, he changed his stroke, driving his paddle deep, then turning it outward to maintain a shred of rudder control. For a few moments longer, he wanted to believe there would be an escape.

Suddenly—frighteningly—Hanuma's body began to rise in the boat. At first, Dangari thought the old man was helping to ward off the bat.

It looked like he was *standing*.

Finally, Dangari understood. The bat, its wings flopping wildly, had grasped Hanuma by his throat. It held him high, biting violently at Hanuma's neck, holding him aloft like a rag doll.

There came a scream from ahead, and Dangari glimpsed Muras being washed over the falls. Dangari swung his paddle at the bat. He tried to stand and tear the creature's glistening wings, but he was thrown off balance and the dugout capsized.

The bed of palm leaves and ferns scattered about Dangari like confetti and the current seized him. As the river hurled him toward the great drop, he saw a moss-covered rock near the edge. For a second, hope swelled in him, but he was swept past the rock. He saw the overturned pirogue and tried to grab onto it. Perhaps it would become wedged between rocks or sunken branches or . . .

He couldn't hold on.

Preparing to die, Dangari saw what looked like a clump of weeds floating in the current with him. His hands grasped at the long flowing white strands. For an instant they felt like a heavenly silkiness. They made him think of an angel's hair. Delicate hair. Flowing. An angel had come for him. That was his final thought before he glimpsed the open dark mouth and the glint of a gold tooth in the moonlight.

For a moment, the current buoyed him. As he was washed over the brink of the falls, he realized he was clutching Hanuma's severed head.

10 • SOUNDS

D r. Lefkovitz took the first two-hour shift as lookout, feeding the campfires in case the bat decided to come back. The terror of the night and jet lag had knocked Jake out. He fell into a deep sleep.

Several of the younger men worked on their life-size effigies long into the night, until the silhouettes and mud faces looked eerily real in the flickering firelight. Two of the strongest workers took the second shift, and Magyar asked to handle the watch closest to dawn—when he'd have to be up anyway preparing food for the men.

Magyar waited until everyone was asleep before he decided to scout the perimeter of the camp. He found the morning shift more inconvenient than frightening. He hadn't seen the bat himself, and, in truth, he was used to the exaggerations of his tribesmen. They were always coming to him with tales of a ten-foot carp they'd seen in the river, or an alligator as long as a tree. Magyar knew, as a rule, to cut in half the size of any animal or lizard or fish anyone ever claimed to see anywhere.

He'd seen the bodies of the two men, but small bats and ocelots or a jaguar could have inflicted the same mutilations. He knew there was a large bat that had been blamed, but he'd seen as few as a handful of rodents and large beetles devour half a dead human within a day or so. They, too, went for the eyes, the easiest entrances to soft, moist flesh. Carcasses of any sort never lasted long in the jungle.

What Magyar was concerned about was the meat supply for the two weeks remaining before the expedition was to head back to Manaus. As he scouted close to the edge of the jungle, he heard sounds of small animals and, perhaps, night herons scurrying about in the undergrowth. He knew the men would be happy if he could make a fresh kill. A roast tapir or a few large white monkeys would pick up everyone's spirits. He could hear the praise he'd get if he could serve something freshly caught.

One deep rustling caught Magyar's attention where the jungle thickened into a hammock of mangrove trees at the river's edge. There, amid the vines and branches, he'd harvested several large snakes and turtle eggs over the last few weeks. He took a hunting dart from his chest sling, slid it into his blowpipe, and headed into the shadows.

He heard the rustling again.

Magyar could feel his mouth go dry and his pulse begin to quicken. The hunt always excited him, and he was certain he'd outsmart whatever was hiding in the maze and darkness of the mangrove roots. He could already smell the fresh animal flesh cooking on a spit turning over the fire. He knew he'd use the drippings of a fresh monkey or parrot to mix with flour into a blood paste, a delicacy among his tribesmen. He knew a good blood paste would boost everyone's morale, and they would forget about the silly bat.

As a head cook and hunter for many years, his eyesight in darkness was as keen as a river hawk. He took a few steps, then halted and listened. Another step. And another, and then stopped again.

The rustle. The animal breathing. It was still there.

Magyar prided himself on being able to stalk closer to any prey than all of the hunters of his tribe. He wouldn't be a fool. He didn't want to get too far from the light of the fires and the protecting effigies. The rustlings he heard were different from others he'd known. It seemed to be something large. Something crawling. He began to pray for a very large and fat iguana or gecko. He stopped when he saw a dark shape just ahead of him.

A boar, he thought.

He would roast another boar. . . .

Suddenly, the dark shape was moving fast toward him. He was shocked by it swiftness, something reaching him and whisking up from the blackness at his feet. A thought—*What is it?*—shot through Magyar's mind. Whatever the thing was, it rushed up his body, knocking the blowpipe from his lips. It had the weight of a large animal. He opened his mouth to cry out.

To shout . . .

But there was no sound.

No terrible pain.

Only a great pressure at his throat and a cracking

of bone and cartilage. A moment later and he could feel a vise of needle teeth that rendered his jaw frozen. He was on the ground now—on his back—and whatever it was held him down with the force and precision of a puma. Like a jungle cat, it had him by the neck, this thing, this black thing that now began to flap its wings on either side of him.

It took Magyar a moment to realize that the creature that held him was convulsing, the whole of its body shaking, vomiting fluids directly into his throat and mouth and . . .

By now he knew everything Dr. Lefkovitz and Jake and the other workers had said was true. A patch of the night fog had broken straight up to the canopy. Moonlight crashed down through the hammock, and he could see a part of the bat's head. Grotesquely shaped, with wet membranes that unfurled from its nostrils and ears. Dr. Lefkovitz had taught him the anatomy of bats. Magyar stared into the large, intense black eyes.

A moment more, and he knew that whatever the fluids were that the creature was pumping into his throat were drugging him—clouding his mind. They were numbing, dulling all pain now. He was paralyzed.

The bat relaxed and disengaged its teeth from his

neck. It crawled off of him and circled him for a moment. When its full face hovered over him once more, it was staring at him sideways. A long, narrow tongue slid out from between its needle teeth and began to lick Magyar's eyelids.

Magyar felt the moist touch of the tongue.

It was gentle. Cooling.

Absurdly, Magyar felt hope flowing back into his thoughts. He knew that if the saliva was like that of the small vampires, it would slowly dissolve the skin from his face. It would make his cheeks bleed, and the bat would take its time savoring the blood.

It would lick carefully.

With delight.

Slowly.

As he'd seen the smaller bats do with their prey in the canopy.

There would be time, Magyar believed. Time for someone to awaken and realize he was missing from his watch. Dr. Lefkovitz, or one of the men, would look out to the fire and effigies, and realize something was wrong. They'd track him the short distance he'd traveled into the jungle. They would find him. The bat would hear them coming, and it would fly off and away from him.

Suddenly, he saw the bat's mouth open like a constrictor's. The full spectrum of its horrible teeth and crimson-coated gums floated over him now, dripping with what he knew now was his own blood.

No, he thought. *Oh, God . . .*

With a quick burst of saliva, two small openings in the creature's upper gums undulated, and a pair of hollow, sharp fangs began to emerge. They slid downward—seven, eight inches!—and locked into place with the precision of dental drills. Convulsing again, the bat lowered the fangs until they entered Magyar's eyes. Moments later, still conscious—even in blindness—Magyar knew the bat was drinking his mind.

Dr. Lefkovitz awakened as the first light of dawn touched the camp. He went outside expecting to see Magyar cooking breakfast meats and stirring a steaming pot of boiling roots mixed with the dried mushrooms and fish that had been brought up from Manaus. The effigies stood in the morning mist.

"Magyar," Dr. Lefkovitz called softly, near the central fire. All the fires had burned low, but he thought it was just Magyar conserving the logs as dawn had approached. When there was no answer, Dr. Lefkovitz became concerned.

A wind came up from the mountains, and cleared the view to the river. Dr. Lefkovitz decided he'd look for Magyar on the bank. He was always catching fresh river bass and frogs to blend into his soups and pastes. The sun hadn't dried the mud bank, and it was easy to spot the fresh footprints. Dr. Lefkovitz knew about the riches of the mangrove hammock.

"Hey," he called out again. "Magyar."

The mangrove roots rose high above the jungle floor. Several crawling sucker-fish had left the water and climbed into the roots to feed on moths and stick bugs. Dr. Lefkovitz found his sandals sinking into a squishing mud. He was several feet from the bank now, and was afraid the river had begun to rise and swell the watershed and pockets of quicksand— the first sign that the annual flood was imminent.

There was an odor of decay in the air, and it began to sting Dr. Lefkovitz's nostrils. He tried to shake off his sleep, and as he pried his foot loose from the mud, he looked down and noticed the mud had an unusual red tint to it. He stepped back away from it, and felt something cracking beneath his feet. It looked like a white branch. But there were other sprigs of white and—

He realized he was looking at pieces of a skull.

At first he thought they were from some animal, but then he saw a rib cage. It looked human—but barely—and it was only the shape of the jawbone that gave it away. Dr. Lefkovitz began to call out, to shout, as he realized he was standing in the middle of something very bad. The flecks of bone and flesh were sprayed across the mud like confetti. He saw now that the whole jungle floor was moving, alive with beetles carrying tiny pieces of human flesh to their lairs in the earth and roots and beneath fallen trees.

Even as he shouted to awaken the whole camp, he knew what had happened to Magyar. He understood that—and what would have to be done.

11 • THE TRAP

A half dozen workers were stringing garlands of leaves and shredded bamboo over the netting, pulleys, and support ropes, camouflaging the reality that the new addition to the riverwalk was, in truth, a trap.

"Tighter," Dr. Lefkovitz was shouting to Rasdyr, the smallest of the workers, who could climb to the very top of the canopy's thinnest branches. "Pull the ropes tighter."

Rasdyr, his body already dripping in the hot morning sun, smiled broadly and signaled that he understood.

"How does it work?" Jake asked his father when he came up in the sling. "It looks like some kind of jerryrigged batting cage."

"It's basically a room made of very strong rope and jungle vines," his father said. "When that monster returns, it will have to land at the end of the riverwalk and crawl forward." Jake followed his father inside the rope chamber. "One end of the trap will be left open."

"How do you know it'll come in?" Jake asked.

"There will be something it wants inside."

"What?"

"Bait."

"What kind?"

"Human."

Jake glared at his father. "Dad, didn't that thing kill enough people? Who's going to be nuts enough to be in here?"

"I'll be in the trap," his father said. "Rasdyr and I." He pointed to the opening. "When the bat crawls in, it'll trip a rope trigger that'll fly two additional nets into place, sealing the trap and dividing the chamber. We'll be safe in this half. The bat will be trapped in the other half. We can fire darts into it until it falls unconscious."

"*Unconscious?*"

"Yes," his father said, stripping his voice of any emotion. "I want to capture it alive."

Jake knew his father was fighting to contain a swell of fear and hate and vengeance. "Why alive?" he asked.

"Jake, you've got to realize what all this might mean for the expedition," his father said. "For the museum. We could study the creature. Use it. Learn from it. We have no idea what its biology and behavior can tell us. How does its brain work? What is its chemistry?"

"It ate the brains out of a few of your men," Jake said. "Didn't that tell you enough? At least it's a hint!"

"We could know more. . . ."

"Dad, you're not a trapper or hunter!"

"I used net traps in Indonesia long before you were born, son," his father said. "I developed them for a British zoological project to save the orangutans in the Javanese jungles. An adult male orangutan has the strength of two or three men—they are ferociously strong. You corner a primate like that and it's capable of ripping the arms off you. These net traps worked just fine. We saved over forty—fifty!—orangutans by catching them and relocating them deeper into the jungle and out of the reach of poachers."

"Dad, there's still time for us to leave. Don't you really think that's what we should do?" Jake asked. "We could load the pirogues and be out of here before the night. . . ."

His father didn't answer him. He took Jake down in the sling to the jungle floor. Two of the workers were loading a single pirogue with fresh supplies. "I want you to leave," his father said.

"I'm not going with them," Jake said.

His father took him into the main hut. He pointed to Jake's belongings on the floor next to his cot. "You've got to pack. You're coming here was a mistake, son. I knew there was danger. . . ."

"Is all of this your ego, Dad?" Jake said. "Just so everyone back at the museum might say, 'Oh, boy, Lefkovitz caught a big bat.' It's like you're trying to be a control freak with nature. You want to be bigger than God."

"No, I'm not trying to play God," his father objected.

"Well, a lot of you scientists are," Jake said. "You can just imagine what they'd do with this bat."

"No . . ."

"I think you do."

"Son, when I decided to become a scientist—that

meant I had to follow the research frontier wherever it took me. I and millions of people might be dead. We've always lived on one cutting edge or another. That's what a scientist does. That's what I do. Just because I'm here in the Amazon, it's no different. There will be things we'll learn from this bat. From it's behavior and chemistry and genes. We have a chance here, Jake. . . ."

"A chance for what?"

"I don't expect you to understand."

"You can't go around doing whatever you want, Dad. It's all gone too far. What will you or some experimenting whacko do with this monster's genes? Clone big bats as food supply? Splice its genetic material into farm animals so we can have bigger chickens and goats? Maybe thirty-pound tomatoes!"

"That's absurd. . . ."

"Dad, you're a scientist! You're not supposed to be messing up the environment like everybody else. Walk away from this one. You have to stop them from ruining the Amazon. From killing the rain forests. You can't open a can of worms like this giant bat. Leave it. You'll wreck this whole place! God, Pops, don't mess with this bat. Let's get out of here!"

Exhausted, Jake's father sat on the edge of his cot. For a few moments he stared at Jake, then moved his gaze to the stack of specimen jars, a ray of sunlight cutting through them so the faces of the creatures appeared cruel and macabre. For the first time in his life, Jake's father had no quick dismissal for him. "I think you'd better show me your Gizmo," his father said, quietly. "I'd like to see what it is."

A small smile crept onto Jake's face. "Sure, Dad," he said. "Sure."

"I know it translates sound reflections into images," his father said.

Jake moved quickly and turned Gizmo on. "It does a lot more than that. I had wanted to show you all it could do, but you wouldn't listen." Its narrow rectangular screen glowed. Jake fumbled through his box of equipment, grabbed a wide elastic headband, and attached it to the thin ends of the screen. He placed the lit viewing screen against his forehead.

"This is the fantastic part, Dad. The images that appear on the screen can be sensed on my brow," Jake said. "On anyone's forehead. I can tell the rough shape of objects in total darkness, even with my eyes closed. With training, a human being can use this device to see like a bat!"

"Is that possible?"

"This isn't science fiction," Jake said. "It's *fact*. They're using devices like Gizmo with blind people. I got the idea from *Scientific American*. There are lots of articles about it all over the place now. You've just been too busy down here to keep up with the new stuff."

"Jake, I still want you to leave. . . ."

"But I'm the only one here that's trained to be able to 'see' with this thing. It takes practice. Weeks—months!—like I had preparing for the science fair. Dad, that bat is very, very smart. You need me and Gizmo with you."

Suddenly, there were cries and shouts from outside the hut. Jake and his father rushed outside. Several of the workers had hurried to meet a man staggering out of the jungle toward them. It was a moment before Jake and his father realized it was Muras, covered with mud and blood.

"It followed us. . . ." Muras was screaming. He saw Dr. Lefkovitz and started toward him. The men put their arms around Muras and helped him over the final distance. "It killed Hanuma. The thing, the big bat killed him and Dangari. It followed us!"

Muras collapsed in Dr. Lefkovitz's arms.

Jake ran and got his father's medicine kit. Rasdyr brought water from the trough. As Dr. Lefkovitz cleaned the scrapes and cuts on Muras's body, the workers began to panic and weep. Several shouted angrily at the sky and the jungle and the failed effigies. They cried out with rage and grief.

"Now I've got to stay," Jake told his father. "The bat isn't going to let anyone leave. You know that now, don't you, Dad? *Don't you?*"

"Yes," his father said. "I know it."

12 • WAITING . . .

By nightfall Rasdyr, Jake, and his father had settled in at the back of the trap. The three of them remained silent for a long while. Jake knew that each of them was thinking of Magyar and Hanuma and Dangari in their graves.

Rasdyr was barely five feet tall and, at twenty-eight, still looked more like a boy than a man. His slight build reminded Jake of the jockeys he'd seen on the occasions when his father had taken him along with a few of his colleagues for a day at Yonkers trotter racetrack.

The Indian sat in the middle of the riverwalk platform, which formed the floor of the bat trap. He had separated his darts into two separate small piles. One set of darts had been dipped in a drug mixture distilled from the sap of wildflowers and eucalyptus trees. The others were coated with a mixture concentrated from oleander roots, a poison capable of slaying the largest of tapirs and wild boar.

"Check and recheck everything," Dr. Lefkovitz said. "When the bat comes, we won't have much time."

Jake held back tears as he checked and rechecked the battery belt and wire connections that powered Gizmo. He was remembering gentle, little Hanuma, with his long gray hair and the gold tooth, waiting for him at the airport in Manaus. Jake had respected the no-nonsense approach Hanuma had taken with him. Throughout all their bantering in the taxi and while traveling upriver, there had always been a wisdom and great sweetness in Hanuma's eyes and words.

"Why did the bat have to stalk Hanuma?" Jake asked his father.

"There are many predators—lions and tigers, some of the sharks, humans for that matter—who can sense a pecking order in another species. It has to have been watching us. We'll never know for certain. It can hear our voices. The tones we use. It probably knew Hanuma was high in the pecking order around here."

Jake felt a mixture of fear and vengeance. "It will come back tonight, won't it, Dad?"

"I think so," his father said softly.

"Now I want us to settle the score," Jake said slowly. "I want us to get even."

Rasdyr and his father nodded. One look into Jake's eyes and they knew what anguish he was feeling.

Dr. Lefkovitz, had given strict instructions for the men at the camp to keep the fires burning high and to cluster together until the night was over. He believed the effigies and noise and light would drive the bat to the bait on the riverwalk.

"It's like we're in a trap within a trap," Jake said. "That bat isn't going to be happy until it kills us all. We're already trapped at the camp."

For a while, Dr. Lefkovitz kept a Coleman lamp lit at the center of the trap. He and Rasdyr checked all the knots and pulleys. Jake kept Gizmo trained toward the opening and riverwalk where the bat could enter.

"What if the trip rope doesn't work?" Jake asked.

"That thing wouldn't think twice about charging all three of us."

"It'll work," Dr. Lefkovitz said.

There were the sounds of something moving in the blackness of the riverwalk where the platform stretched out above the river and the light from the Coleman paled.

"Monkeys," Rasdyr said.

Jake nodded. He could see the shapes clearly on Gizmo. They were small ones—several of them. Marmosets, perhaps, or a family of woollys.

Dr. Lefkovitz held a machete ready. For the first time, Jake saw that his father was frightened. Rasdyr slid one of the drug-tipped darts into a blowpipe. He had already loaded several of the reserve pipes and had laid them out neatly in front of him, like a surgeon's tools. Faint vapors from the sap had risen and mixed with the sweat on his face. He scratched with his long fingernails at the irritated skin on his cheeks and forehead.

By three in the morning, Rasdyr appeared tired and in need of a nap. He had worked hard all day preparing the darts and carving the blowpipes. Occasionally a strong wind would blow off the river, and the jungle mist and fog would clear. Then the fires and lean-tos of the camp could be glimpsed far beneath them.

"Who taught you how to hunt?" Jake asked Rasdyr.

"My father taught me how to stay alive in the jungle." Rasdyr tried to smile. He took water from a canteen and splashed it on his face.

Soon they could see the moon directly above them. The treetops were aglow, silver and shimmering. Dr. Lefkovitz turned off the Coleman, and the three waited in silence again. They could hear the gurgling sounds of the river and see it sparkle like a thick glittering ribbon below and south of the walkway.

Dr. Lefkovitz moved slowly closer to the center of the trap. He listened to every peep and chirp and gentle crackling of the canopy.

There was a loud whooshing somewhere ahead, and Jake felt a chill crawl up his neck and across his scalp. There were new smells in the canopy now: dust, and a jasmine fragrance in the air. The late hour and crisp moonlight began to play tricks with his eyes and blur his vision. His mind was racing. All the death and loss that had happened was beginning to shift and seep into places in his brain and heart where he couldn't escape it.

Jake realized that the three of them were waiting like cheese in a mousetrap. He sat to the left of Rasdyr on a bed of leaves camouflaging the walkway. Panic swelled in him until he felt as if he were in a speeding car about to crash. There was the scream of a river loon. His stomach hardened into a knot.

Suddenly, the chattering and whirring of monkeys and insects disappeared. An utter stillness fell on the canopy, so that the only sound was the faint march of the river as it washed against the banks and churned downstream into white water.

More silence.

Dr. Lefkovitz had heard a silence like this before when he had been in Java and the lush mountains of Kenya. It was a silence that preceded the arrival of the king of a vast primate colony. That's how it had been with the monkeys and apes: first, a shrieking that froze one's heart; and then an utter, uncanny silence while all the lesser monkeys awaited the appearance of the royal apes in the pecking order.

A breeze crept into the canopy. Jake saw an image fluttering at the center of Gizmo's screen.

"Dad, it's coming."

His father moved closer to watch the ghostly

electronic picture. The night mist had conjured itself once more, thick enough to blacken out the moonlight. Now the men heard something in the sky.

A thing soaring overhead.

A few moments later, they heard it again. The glide of a large airborne creature closing in.

There were vibrations now. The platform shaking. The creature had landed on the platform ahead of them. For a moment, the vague image disappeared from the screen and there were new sounds behind them. Then to the left and right.

Jake shifted, and redirected Gizmo. It was when he turned to check the trap's opening that he noticed the shadow, as if a large tree branch were moving in a breeze. Rasdyr coughed. A moment later, the stench reached Jake's nostrils. His father had already covered his mouth. It was the horrid smell of rotting meat, like chicken that had stayed weeks too long in its package.

There came a wheezing sound, and the shadow crawled forward.

13 • ENCOUNTER

A sliver of moonlight broke through again. Now Jake could see the reflection in the pair of huge glass eyes that stared at him. He saw the wet, dripping snout of the huge chiropteran lifted up into the night breeze. It sniffed fiercely. Intensely.

Catching the full lure of the scent of human flesh, the shadow continued forward. The boards of the platform creaked beneath its weight. Even without the aid of Gizmo now, they could see the bat bunched up. It appeared to be the size of a small car. As one of its wings lifted from its body, Jake thought the bat must surely have passed the trip rope—the waiting trigger of jungle vine, fishing catgut, and rope. One wing moved so that it protruded to the left. The bat crawled closer still.

"It should be *now*," Rasdyr whispered.

The bat stopped.

Jake's eyes had become accustomed to the night and darkness and the shadows of the moonlight. He could see the bat swiveling its head as if sensing something wrong. Dangerous. It lifted its head and sniffed again toward the three figures crouched at the far end of the vine cluster. It decided to proceed. As it did, its talons dragged across the trip rope.

There was the quick pivoting of rope and pulleys, a dropping of log weights on either side of the net which made the inner mesh rise with a scream. Guy wires screeched, and the bat shuddered with surprise. The netting at the center of the room was in place now, and the entrance behind the bat was sealed. The bat was caught inside the rope cage.

As the final counterweights pulled taut the top of the trap, the bat sat midway between the platform railings. It watched the physics of the entrapment, swiveling its head from left to right. When all the sounds had halted, it gazed toward the net roof with what looked more like curiosity than fear.

Jake and Rasdyr, stood frozen, amazed that the

trap had worked. They stared through the net divider at the freakish creature looking back at them. They could see the bat's eyes. Its every instinct was focused on them.

There was a snorting that deepened into a wheezing. The bat's jaws opened like a mouth-breather's, and a hot froth dripped from the its lips.

Jake gasped. He could see the bat more objectively now than in the madness of the first night when it had attacked Hanuma. It seemed to stare at the glow of Gizmo in his hands, and then lifted its lazy gaze and fixed its eyes on him. Jake's pulse quickened, as he became convinced that the bat remembered him.

The bat twisted its head to the right, keeping one dark, terrible eye on Jake. The reek of its mouth announced the mark of the carnivore, and its wheezing transmuted into a hissing sound like a massive cobra. It moved forward, its taloned feet dragging along the planking like those of a gargoyle come to life on the edge of an ancient rampart.

It turned one ear in the direction of Gizmo, with its piercing electronic sounds.

Instinctively, Jake moved nearer to his father, who held a machete ready. Dr. Lefkovitz took the full measure of the maze of thick arteries and veins that had developed in the creature's wings, making them resemble the spokes of an enormous open umbrella. Winged beetles and tropical cicadas buzzed and clustered around the bat's face, attracted to its rancid smells and specks of rotting carrion.

For a moment longer, the two sides—the bat and the men—stared at each other in disbelief.

The bat stood up on its legs and spread its wings to their full span—twenty, twenty-five feet! It began to screech with a volume that shook the entire platform. It launched itself violently into the air, flying straight at the dividing net.

Rasdyr, Jake, and Dr. Lefkovitz rushed back and away as the screaming bat crashed into the netting in front of them. The net stretched forward, its ropes extending until all slack was gone. The anchor branches strained and creaked like long, brittle fingers. It seemed certain the ropes would snap.

But they held.

The bat slammed its feet back down onto the platform. Its head swiveled on its hairy, thick neck. It hissed its outrage again and its stinking, scalding breath rolled toward the men. Its forelimbs boasted another set of talons that had atrophied into a comb of thick barbs. Like a rioting bird of prey, it screamed its ire through its dagger fangs.

It shuddered and rose up again. The ropes squeaked under the savage strain. But the bat was caught. Perplexed. Furious.

Its talons shot forward and down, testing the ropes and planking for a weakness. Jake, his father, and Rasdyr were stunned by the bat's ferocity. The bat hurled itself against the netting like a crazed ram, its hooked claws reaching out to cut them. Savage them. Kill and feed!

Jake checked the peak of the net, where the ropes drew to a nexus like the top of a circus tent. The riverwalk platform quaked violently—but still the netting and wooden boards held. The bat seized the net in its teeth and shook it like an angry dog with a pull toy. Leaves and fruit and beetles rained down from the highest domain of the canopy. All the small living things crawled and dropped off the edge, plummeting toward the jungle floor.

Jake and his father looked at each other.

"NOW!" his father shouted.

Rasdyr began to fire the drug-tipped darts. The first hit the bat's face. The second stuck in the bat's pug nose—and another hit the flesh above its left eye. The bat shrieked with renewed rage, and clawed at the darts until he had scraped them off.

Dr. Lefkovitz dropped down on his knees next to Rasdyr, grabbed another of the loaded blowpipes, and helped fire off a second spray of darts. Rasdyr, too, fired again and again. The bat shook, screeched raucously, and bit wildly at the net that separated it from its attackers.

"I want the bat alive," Dr. Lefkovitz shouted. "I need it *alive*."

14 • THE DEATH OF RASDYR

Jake, too, grabbed a blowpipe and managed to fire a drug-tipped dart into the bat's face. The bat stared maliciously at Jake and shrieked deafeningly. The violent fluttering and clawing of the bat was so alarming, even Rasdyr wasn't able to shoot straight. The darts began to miss their mark.

"Stop firing," Dr. Lefkovitz shouted. "Don't provoke it anymore. Let the drug take effect."

The bat quieted and backed away from the division net. It checked the trap entrance, clawed at it. But that was sealed, too.

The bat turned back to look at them. Rasdyr held another dart ready to fire, and moved closer to the net dividing the space.

"Be careful," Dr. Lefkovitz said.

The bat was standing up now. It was eerily quiet, checking every inch of the trap with its dark, mucous-rimmed eyes.

Rasdyr could see that the darts were taking their toll. On various hunts, he had seen several tapirs and enraged jaguars succumb slowly to the drug's power. The bat appeared to be drifting toward sleep. It looked mesmerized, riveted.

Rasdyr moved closer to the division net and the creature. He picked up another of the drug-tipped darts, loaded a blowpipe, and held it aimed toward the bat's eyes. If the dart could strike the flesh of an eye, the drug would flow quickly to its brain—even make it collapse. From experience, he had learned the amount of the wildflower-eucalyptus sap that would cause a large animal to close its eyes and drop unconscious.

"Don't go too close," Dr. Lefkovitz warned Rasdyr.

But Rasdyr was already dangerously near the division net. He raised the blowpipe into position. As he inhaled deeply to propel the dart through the long slender tube, the massive bat exploded into motion again. It came hurtling at the divider.

The force of the collision stretched the net farther than anyone had thought possible. The forelimb
claws of the bat ripped through the net and grasped
Rasdyr. The claws tore into Rasdyr's shoulders, and
blood from an artery shot out like water from a
shower hose. Jake and Dr. Lefkovitz reached forward
quickly. They each reflexively grabbed one of
Rasdyr's arms, and tried to yank him back out of
harm's way—but they were no match for the savage
strength of the bat.

"EEEEH! EEEEEEEH!"

Rasdyr cried out as the bat flexed its talons, digging them deep until they surrounded solid muscle
tissue and bone. It pulled Rasdyr violently to its breast
now—at the same time leaping upward and digging
the claws of its feet into the top of Rasdyr's midsec-
tion. Like a huge dark ostrich, it kicked its powerful
legs downward. Rasdyr's whole abdomen burst open.

Instantly, Rasdyr was dead.

It was several moments before Jake and his father
fully understood that they were holding the arms of
a disemboweled corpse.

"Let him go," Dr. Lefkovitz shouted—to himself
as well as Jake.

They released their grasp on Rasdyr's arms. The

bat shrieked and tore farther through the net into the chamber. It let loose Rasdyr's bloody body, and dropped down onto it. It tore at the dead face and neck and chest, not feeding or devouring. It used its teeth to slice and dismember.

Instinctively Jake threw open the volume switch on Gizmo.

BEEP BEEP BEEP.

The electronic blaring had confused the monster on the night that it had grabbed Hanuma. Now, delirious with horror, Jake somehow hoped it would give him and his father the seconds they needed to escape.

His father had spun around and was hacking with his machete at the vine they'd used to secure an exit flap at the rear of the trap. The bat's rage was focused on Jake and Gizmo now. Its nostrils dripped with a green ooze as it shook the netting and managed to thrust its cruel, snapping jaws farther through the rip of the netting. Its flailing claws scooped and swung inches from Jake's legs.

As the bat rolled its head and screamed audibly in a shaft of moonlight, its talons reached deep, pawing through the sad remains of what was Rasdyr. Suddenly, it grasped the palm-wood planks of the trap floor itself. It spread its wings with a power and turbulence that tore the division net wide open, and it stepped through the entrails toward Jake.

The trap was only a shattered spiderweb when Dr. Lefkovitz gave a final slash. The exit flap fell open, and Jake crawled out. Jake's father was quick behind him—and they were running. A second later, the bat's head and wings crashed through the rupture, and it was after them.

"The sling," Dr. Lefkovitz called out.

Jake ran toward the center platform. The sling to descend was waiting. It would hold both of them. Jake reached it. He leaped into it and held it against the railing, ready to launch.

"Hurry up," he shouted to his father.

Dr. Lefkovitz rushed toward him. The bat was crawling—racing—swiftly, half-flying after him. Jake held the sling open. For a moment, he met his father's terrified gaze and knew he had made another decision.

"Save yourself," his father said.

"No!" Jake cried out.

Then his father was at the sling. The bat was coming fast. Jake turned the volume of Gizmo up still higher. The loud beeping was earsplitting, but it didn't slow the bat.

"Don't!" Jake said, as his father reached out for the sling release. It was too late. His father sent Jake and the sling descending toward the jungle floor. Horrified, Jake watched his father sidestep onto the north catwalk. The bat halted to see Jake and the retreating sling—then the bat chose another, a crueller, turn.

There was shouting from the camp as the men realized that something had gone terribly wrong at the trap.

"The bat's after my dad!" Jake shouted as he reached the bottom.

Jake leaped out of the sling. He took off beneath the path of the north walkway, straining to see up through a mesh of tropic evergreens and moonlight. The men, with cries of fear, raced along beside him.

There was a scream from above.

There came the sounds of a heavy weight crashing down from the canopy—something falling through the layers of delicate branches and strands of fleshy orchids and vines. There was the thud of a body hitting the sea of red clay and broadleafs that were the jungle floor.

15 • VENGEANCE

Frightened and shouting, the Indian men hacked their way through the jungle undergrowth and reached the fallen body first. Sorgno, the young man who could speak only broken English, grabbed Jake and led him to the spot. "Your father. Hurt."

Sorgno led Jake to where the group of men had gathered. Jake knew how far his father had fallen. He had heard the branches crack, breaking his father's fall as he smashed down through them.

The men stepped aside to make room for Jake. Some of the Indians had terror in their eyes; others had sorrow.

He walked to the center of the group of men, and dropped down on his knees next to his father. His father was covered with bruises and wounds.

Capillaries on his arms had burst, and his eyes were closed. His face and hair were cloaked in blood, and his left leg stuck out in an impossible direction. A chunk of white bone protruded from the skin of his knee.

Jake saw his father's chest rise and fall, and heard his troubled breathing. Each breath was a hard wheezing. A struggle. He started coughing and a strand of blood dripped out the side of his mouth. Jake was afraid his father was dying in front of him.

But that mustn't be.

"Get a cot," Jake yelled. He reinforced with a mime of what was needed. "Something flat. Hurry."

Sorgno translated. Three of the men left for the lean-tos. Taking off his own shirt to use as a towel, Jake wiped the dirt and blood off his father's face. He took his father's hand and whispered in his ear: "Don't worry, Dad—you'll be okay. We'll get you out of here." Jake turned to Sorgno. "We have to get his bone back inside," Jake said. "Set it as best we can."

"I have done this," Sorgno said. "I can do it."

The men returned with a cot. They gently lifted Jake's father onto it and carried it like a stretcher to the main hut.

"My dad needs a doctor," Jake said to Sorgno. "He has to get down to the Fathers' village. To the missionaries. Muras needs treatment, too. They'll have to radio for a helicopter or my dad will die. I want your best rowers—the strongest river men—in their pirogues, and they've got to leave *now*."

"We cannot leave on the river," Sorgno said. "They will be slaughtered like Hanuma and Dangari. We must carry Dr. Lefkovitz and Muras through the jungle."

"How long would that take?" Jake asked.

"Three days, maybe more."

"My dad doesn't have three days," Jake said, his patience running out. "Can't you see he's dying? Do you want me to paddle him down there myself? Is that what I have to do?" Jake shouted.

"The bat will get him," Sorgno said. "We will not go on the river."

Jake's eyes filled with rage, and he shoved Sorgno to the ground. Furiously, he drew back his fist to punch him, but Sorgno was faster, stronger. He grabbed Jake's fists and stopped them from striking him. An older Indian cried out from the doorway.

"Stop!" Muras said, barely able to stand. "Sorgno is right. As long as the bat lives, your father and our people will never make it past Dark Angel Falls."

Sorgno let Jake get up.

Jake began to choke with anxiety and panic. He fought until he had control again. "If we all go down river in the daytime, we'll be safe."

"No," Muras said. "This bat will not be frightened of daytime. It will leave its darkness. Its roost in the canopy or cave in the river cliffs. Wherever it sleeps. Where it gains strength and readies itself."

Sorgno translated for the men, and they began to cry out fearfully and shout protests in Murdaruci.

"The bat will come after us in the bright sun," Sorgno told Jake what they were saying. "It will not stop until we are all dead."

"You believe that?" Jake asked.

"Yes."

Jake saw that all the men were staring at him. He realized they were looking to him to convince them—to make the right decision. They were riveted on him as he had seen them look to his father and Hanuma.

"Then we're going to have to destroy it," Jake said.

Sorgno told the men what was said. Again they reacted.

"They say that it will not die," Sorgno said. "We are the ones that will be killed."

Dr. Lefkovitz's eyes opened, and he cried out in pain. Jake crouched down at his side. "They'll get you to the village," Jake said. He saw a look in his father's eyes that he had never seen before. "Dad, tell me what to do. Tell me."

His father looked away to the rack of preserved specimens, the hundred or so small black bodies floating—the heads of the bats frozen in fury. He glanced back at Jake.

"I was wrong, son," he said. His voice was weak and it broke with pain and anguish. "Get the men out of here," he said. "Safely out. Leave me. It's my fault. . . ."

For the first time in his life, Jake felt his father was speaking from his heart. He strained to say something more."

"What, Pops?"

"Forgive me for not seeing who you've become, son. Forgive me. . . ."

"It's okay, Dad. . . ."

His father's eyes closed once more, and his breathing quickened.

Jake dipped a cloth in a cup of fresh water, and

wet his father's lips. He knew his father was slipping fast.

"You'll all leave," Jake said decisively to the men. "I'll stay."

Muras sat exhausted on the floor. He saw the hate and the ferocity in Jake's eyes.

All the men knew if they didn't do something, Dr. Lefkovitz would die.

Jake said, "The bat won't follow you if I make noise. If I keep the sounds of the camp going. I'll shout and yell, and make enough noise with Gizmo and my boom box. I'll blast it while you drift quietly away. I'll make a racket that'll make the bat think there are still dozens of us here. Besides, I'm the one it probably really hates now. Me and Gizmo."

"If we leave you here, you will be dead," Sorgno said.

"No," Jake said, determined. "It will be the bat who dies."

The afternoon sun burned off the thick morning fog that had rolled from the river onto the banks. Muras had the men do everything that Jake wanted to prepare for his stand against the bat. They knew if they didn't get the men moving, they'd start defecting anyway.

Once Dr. Lefkovitz had been safely strapped into a pirogue, the fears of the men nearly reached the breaking point. Even Sorgno knew if they all didn't leave together, they'd panic and start taking off alone in a pirogue, or run away—two or three at a time— into the jungle. Divided, the small terrorized groups would be certainly stalked and killed.

Daylight was fleeting. Sorgno and Kiro, the strongest riverman left from the expedition, would take Dr. Lefkovitz in the lead dugout. They prayed there would be safety in numbers and that Jake's plan would work. Jake had packed the medicines, and Sorgno knew how to give an injection if Dr. Lefkovitz went into shock. Jake made Sorgno promise to never leave his father's side as he had never left Hanuma's.

The loading of the half dozen dugouts was done quietly and under the cover of the mangrove trees at the left of the small beach. The loud sounds of the camp at work were simply just that—sounds. The only thing moving in the camp was the tape deck of Jake's boom box. With its volume on ten, it seemed like the whole camp was booming with the ordinary sounds of chopping and cooking and preparing for a night research trip into the canopy.

Jake gently and silently helped the men edge the last pirogue into the water. On board was Dr. Lefkovitz bundled up and strapped in like a mummy, but miraculously still alive.

Muras was the last to whisper to Jake. "Be careful," he whispered.

Jake nodded. He watched the men frozen still, holding their paddles, as they began the drift along the downstream bank under the cover of thick, arching palms and stilt roots. The current began to move the cluster of pirogues silently, secretly, down river.

Several of the men looked back at Jake. He saw the expressions on their faces, and decided it was a mixture of terror and profound sadness. It was as if they knew for certain that it would be the last time they'd ever see him alive.

Jake waited by the river for a long while after the boats had disappeared around the first bend. He listened to the noisy, coughing truck motor. He could see the silver flash of the large schools of piranha feeding on frogs and catfish along the far bank. The vibrations of the truck motor still kept them away from the camp beach.

As Jake walked back up the bank he hoped the blasting recorded sounds of the workers and rock music would be enough to keep the bat fooled that all was business as usual at the camp.

It was strange walking through the empty camp, but sounds from the truck motor and tape deck comforted him. He found himself thinking, *You'll be okay, Dad. Even when the bat knows it's only me and Gizmo here, that'll probably be enough to keep it here for a while. Sorgno and Muras and the men will have you safely at the village. . . .*

Then he remembered the sight of his father bleeding and broken on the floor of the jungle, and he clenched his fists. He caught himself gasping, breathing fitfully. He knew his eyes were wide with fear—as if the bat were already attacking. As the full realization that he was alone, he found himself stumbling, fighting for breath.

He looked down and saw the image of himself reflected in the drinking trough. He stared, mesmerized by his image. His hair and face were speckled with river mud. He brushed the dirt from his forehead, as if to make certain he was truly seeing himself.

He rubbed at his eyes, and a wave of realization

rushed up and overwhelmed him. He turned and looked up into the failing light, at the treeline and labyrinth of the canopy. Slowly, a look of vengeance and hatred crossed over his face and he continued his preparations to meet the bat.

16 • NIGHT OF THE BAT

The sun was setting fast along the Amazon. Clouds of mosquitoes rose from the river banks and giant aruanas leaped out of the water to catch baby lizards scurrying across vast stretches of giant lily pads.

Before they left, the men had helped Jake construct what he had chosen as his final defense against the bat, if all else failed. Unlike his father, he knew he mustn't underestimate the power and intelligence of the bat. His father's trap had been recast into a large rectangular net that stretched so that it extended out over the river. The dozen human effigies from the camp were reinforced with bamboo and clay, and brought up to the riverwalk. Under Jake's instructions, two of the best climbers among the men had hung them from vines beneath the netting. They made an eerie mobile above the river, moving in the wind of the canopy.

In the last of the sunlight that angled into the camp, Jake scraped the milky poison from a dozen of Rasdyr's scattered arrows and placed it in the ridges at the end of a single sharp blow-dart he'd whittled. He held the sticky sap over a bed of hot embers until the considerable mass of poison melted and fused solidly onto the tip.

Jake hoped that if he got the chance to fire this single dart with its megadose of poison—if he could make its tip rip fast and hard into the bat's underbelly or deep into an eye—that the poison would kill. Or blind. At least slow the bat. But he couldn't be sure.

By dusk, he had the last of his supplies out of the main hut and struggled to pull himself up by the sling. On this trip up into the canopy, he was loaded with a drum of gasoline and as many pots as he could tie onto the pulleys. These, too, would be part of his master plan.

He had had Sorgno and the other men strip the electric wiring from the north walkway, and help him wrap it around one of the effigies. Jake rigged it with a separate line run from the generator and wired in a length of metal stripping to fashion a switch. Sorgno had beached a single pirogue for him, the smallest.

If he were alive to use it.

As Jake pulled himself higher, pain flared up from blisters on his hands. He looked out across the tops of the canopy and saw the last of the bright gold and purple clouds of the sky. On another evening he might have paused and looked longer at the sunset. But not tonight. Not now. He promised himself he'd watch it again soon with his dad. Yes, that was a fine thought. They'd be at a restaurant in Manaus, or Belem—or they'd be leaving on a jet back to New York. That thought gave him strength as he continued to pull himself up to the top.

He took the heavy, red drum of gasoline and began to drench the center platform of the canopy. He felt it was the best shot, and he decided he'd use it first. He knew it would depend upon the bat flying toward him. He'd be the living bait at the end of a puddle fuse. The bat would need to be low, flying very low over the fumes when the incendiary pool ignited. The flames could shoot twenty feet in the air. Burn the bat's wings. Set it on fire.

But again, he couldn't be sure.

In a promontory north of the camp—in a cave impossible to see from the ground—a pair of powerful, taloned feet held onto a rock-face. As the sun sunk beneath the horizon of jungle, the wings of the massive bat began to stir. Its eyelids moved and opened, revealing two black shining orbs. A moment more, and its wings stretched wide. Its feet loosened themselves from the rocky cave ceiling—and the bat dropped into flight.

Shrieking filled the air as thousands of smaller bats flew from the main cave in the cliff: the Emergence. Flying among them was what looked like a giant black condor. Its vast wings carried the creature along the river and toward the plumes of smoke from the camp in the distance.

By the light from the string of bulbs surrounding the center platform, Jake finished pouring the gasoline over the wooden octagon. It was the one cleared area where the lush canopy itself wouldn't have a chance of burning. He tossed the empty drum over the side. Seconds later, he heard it hit the jungle floor.

Jake grabbed up two of Magyar's largest cooking pots, a twenty-five gallon soup kettle, and a large aluminum frying pan. He thought of Magyar, and what the bat had done to him, and anger filled his chest. He began to bang the pan lid on the bottom of the kettle. Hard. Crazily. The racket echoed through the night sky and along the river. Jake hoped the bat would want to see what was making the new, violent sounds.

Come and get me. Come . . .

Not far away, the giant bat separated from the main swarm of smaller chiropterans and swooped down, skimming along the tops of the trees.

Jake saw the massive, dark wingspan against the moonlight. The bat was heading right for him. He tossed the pots down onto the platform and waited.

When the bat was less than a hundred yards away, Jake took matches from his pocket and tried to strike one. It broke against the box. He looked up to see the bat above him now, shrieking like a massive bird of prey. With his hand shaking, Jake grabbed another match from the box and scraped it against the box. Its tip burst into a small flame. He heard the swishing of the bat's wings as he tossed the match into a narrow trail of gasoline leading to the soaked platform.

Jake ducked as the bat swooped lower, uncurling its claws and opening its mouth. Suddenly, the gasoline trail hit the main pool and exploded into a lagoon of fire. The bat veered away, but the flames surrounded it. Jake heard its first cry of surprise, which turned into earsplitting shrieks of agony.

The bat flew out of the fire, its abdomen and wings singed. The moisture on its snout boiled and the tips of its wings were charred. The bat was wounded, angrier than ever, as it flew toward him. Jake dove as the bat's talons dragged right over him.

Jake ran away from the fire onto the shadowy riverwalk. He cried out in terror as he glanced back. The gasoline fire had failed. The bat was still after him. He tripped, rolled up onto his feet, and took off, slogging through the veil of vines and along the moss-covered railings. He spun and stumbled again, this time turning his ankle, then scuttling like a crab onto the rotting planking over the river.

The bat made a wide circle. It had no problem finding Jake as he sprinted away. It extended the giant claws of its feet. As the creature bore down on him, Jake made a flying leap off the darkened end of the walkway and grabbed on to a rope wrapped around the trunk of a balsa tree.

The bat slowed its flight and fluttered in a circle around the girth of the tree. In the darkness, it picked up a human silhouette on its sonar and flew right for it. Its front claws and jaws clamped down onto it, and it began to rip the form apart. It hadn't noticed the metal stripping and wires that connected the effigy to the dangling bulb sockets.

The creature screeched as a bolt of electricity shot out from the wired effigy. The bat's muscles contracted and released as the pulsing hot voltage burned into it. It threw itself backward and away from the rigged effigy. The bat fluttered and floundered down into the shadows of the walkway. Jake swung around from the other side of the tree, a machete in his hand.

As he charged at the dazed bat, the smell of rotting flesh mixed with the stench of the creature's burned hair filled Jake's nostrils. He saw lesions and blood on the ruptured skin of the bat's wings and ears. As Jake closed on the bat, he raised the machete above one of the creature's wings.

With an explosive squawk, the bat sprang to life.

Its eyes glared right up at Jake, and its wings shot forward, smashing into his arm. The machete flew out of Jake's hand and over the edge of the walkway. Jake tottered and grabbed the handrail. As he steadied himself, he felt a pain in his arm. The bat had carved a slice into his wrist. Holding onto the cut, Jake took off running again. Ahead of him was a dead end, and behind him was the bat.

Furious, the bat took flight.

At the end of the walkway, Jake quickly slid himself out along one of the dozen ropes that spiderwebbed across the river. He reached a second effigy he had set, one that hung this time in the midst of a dozen like it—the mobile of effigies. Jake looked back, grabbed for his Gizmo and the power belt. He fastened the belt fast around his waist and strapped Gizmo's screen onto his forehead. In the blackness of night he needed to be the equal of the bat.

The moon was blotted out by clouds and the night fog. A strong wind blew across the Amazon. Jake could see nothing with his eyes, but Gizmo's beep-and-retrieve system was coming in clear. He had to remember what it was like to concentrate as he'd trained himself for so many months to see like the blind— to "see" the sound pictures of terror.

17 • FINAL STALKING

Jake heard the noises of the bat, its terrible shrieking. Its sounds confused the images on Gizmo, and Jake struggled to make sense of everything. He looked down toward the water far below. He knew that if he fell he probably wouldn't survive.

The bat swung into the dead end of the walkway and spotted a human silhouette. It flew at the figure and smashed it with its mighty claws. But it smashed only an effigy. The bat knew the difference between crushing wood and crushing human flesh.

The bat sent its sonar out across the spiderwebbing ropes and picked up human silhouettes hanging from half a dozen branches that stretched out over the river. The monster flew to the next effigy and grabbed it, smashing it to splinters. It flew to the next and smashed that into pieces, too.

From behind the effigy he clung to, Jake saw the bat viciously, systematically make its way among the branches, destroying effigy after effigy. He looked out to the netting he'd stretched and set as a trap above the river.

The giant bat smashed an effigy only a few branches away.

Jake took the blowpipe from his holster. He carefully removed the special dart he'd prepared from its hollow bamboo shield and slid it into the tip of the blowpipe. The bat landed on the effigy next to Jake, and he watched its fingerlike spiked claws pulverize the wood and branches.

Jake brought the blowpipe to his mouth. The giant bat flew to the branch above him, and lowered itself to Jake's effigy. As the creature spun the effigy around, it was surprised to see the figure clinging to it.

Summoning all his breath, Jake aimed as best he could, and blew into the blowpipe. The dart flew out from the blowpipe and sunk into the tender, hairy underbelly of the bat. Shrieking, the bat flailed at itself, quickly knocking the dart loose. There couldn't have been enough time for the delivery of a lethal dose.

There was a last chance.

Jake's hands shot up to the pulley line from which his effigy hung. He yanked himself free of the effigy, and dangled. A second later and he was propelling himself, hand over hand, farther out over the river. As his momentum carried him, he wanted the bat to see the glow of Gizmo. He wanted the killer to follow him now with great speed.

This time there was nowhere to hide. The bat swung in and headed for Jake. It knew it had him. The bat raised its wings and thrust its claws forward.

Jake was under the net he'd had the men rig over the river. He turned up the *beep beep* of Gizmo. He wanted the bat to fly into place beneath the rope web.

The bat was screeching, outraged circling around Jake.

"Fly over here and get me!" Jake yelled. "I'm waiting for you! Come on, you big cowardly chicken!"

The bat flew straight at him. The creature came fast, and Jake yanked the trigger vine. He'd planned that there would be time to pull himself clear—to be out from under the net as it fell like a cloak onto the creature's head and wings.

But his hands were slippery with sweat. His grip failed, and now the net was falling onto him *and the bat*. The night mist had moved on a breath of wind, and Jake kicked out at the bat, but the wide, weighted net was already covering both of them. It trapped the two of them, and they began to fall.

Jake screamed.

Like a torn parachute, the fluttering wings of the shrieking bat slowed their fall, but they hit the surface of the river with a great splash. Jake felt the pain on his back, as if he'd landed very badly off a high diving board.

The bat's wings, ebony and streaked with blood, loomed over him. He and the bat began to go under.

They both shuddered and gasped desperately for air, struggling to free themselves from the net. Their cries were chilling, frenzied, and Jake was certain they'd drown. For a stark and eternal second, Jake and the bat's eyes met.

Now—suddenly!—the bat was biting fiercely at the net, fighting to tear it with its teeth and talons. Jake shouted, wanting only to keep clear of the gnashing teeth. He threw off Gizmo and the power belt, and tried to dive under the net, to find a way out by going deeper.

The trap held firm, and when Jake surfaced, the moonlight was dazzling. He could see that the bat had managed to put a long tear in the net. He grabbed for the opening and emerged free into the current. Jake swam toward the sound of the truck motor, toward the camp, and didn't look back until he was closing on the shore. His feet touched the muddy bottom.

– Exhausted, he made his way slowly into the shallows. When he was closer, he thought to look behind him. There was no sign of the net or the bat. A rejoicing began to fill his heart. He began to compose a kind of prayer, to shape his amazement at this survival.

The bat was gone. The ordeal was over. . . .

He emerged from the water near the truck chassis and its running engine. He was thankful its gasoline hadn't run out, but he didn't want to think about that. His mind needed to think of nothing. It needed to rest and eat and sleep and—

SPLASH!

Jake spun around. The bat, near shore, had burst upward from the surface like a phoenix. It rose high, so high that Jake thought it would be airborne, as a missile in a sea launch. But the bat hadn't enough strength yet to fly. It fell back onto the surface. The horror was clawing, floundering toward him. With each stab forward of its wings, it gained strength.

Jake thought he might run. He would try to make it to the main hut. But the cough of the truck engine resonated in his brain. Instinctively, his hand shot out and shut off the gas feed, the lifeline to the engine, and the motor stopped.

He looked across to the opposite shore. There was the flickering of silver fish as they easily, speedily, followed the blood trail of the bat. Seconds later, the bat began to shriek in agony. The fish had reached it. The water around the bat began to boil scarlet. The creature desperately, pathetically, swung its wings upward in a last attempt at flight. Dozens of frenzied piranha had already fastened themselves to its skin.

More piranha came, as if the whole river were filled with the hungry fish. The bat's shrieks grew louder and angrier. Finally its cries were hopeless. Its winged forearms became skeletal, its skull was stripped of flesh, and the creature sank, slowly disappearing into the blackness of the river.

For a while Jake rested on the riverbank near the camp. The moon was high, and at the horizon the first glow of dawn began to creep into the sky. By daylight it was clear that the river was rising, and he would have to leave in the last pirogue. A family of sea otters came downstream in the first wave of the flooding. They stopped and played in the slowly drowning mangrove roots, the younger ones sliding down the last crest of the muddy bank. The largest of the otters hunted for fish in the new shallows.

Soon Jake's strength returned, and he started out on the trip home, the trip downstream. The entire camp would be beneath the swelling river. As he launched himself in the pirogue, he could sense in his heart that his father was safe. Somewhere safe. The men would have made it to the village. An army helicopter would have come. His father could even be at the hospital in Manaus.

But there would be many of his father's men, his workers, still at the village when Jake drifted out of the river mist in the small dugout. He knew the workers would be watching for him. They would tell the village. Jake would be embraced by them, and there would be a gathering. There would be a fresh roast boar, and something cold to drink. He would be invited to sit with the men around a campfire. They would sit and listen as he told them about the end of the night of the bat.

ACKNOWLEDGMENTS

Thanks to Arleen Perkins and her Sweetie Pies at Grover Cleveland Middle School for helping me decide between *Night of the Bat* and *Bats* as the title for this book. It was driving me batty.

Also, my appreciation to Janet Walker at St. Mark's School of Texas for launching me into the electronic and encyclopedic literature of the mammalian order of Chiroptera.

And to the Smithsonian Institution for its extraordinary research and photography reporting the scientific benevolence and majesty of bats.

Last, but not least, my gratitude to Francesco, the gentle bat that chose to roost on the ceiling of my porch for the duration of the writing of this book.